SETH

7H THE BROTHERS OF HASTINGS RANCH SERIES
BOOK SEVEN

By Katharine E. Hamilton

ISBN-13: 978-1-735-81259-5

Seth

www.katharinehamilton.com

Cover Design by Kerry Prater.

To West.
My youngest little man.
My little man who loves to be outside, climb
anything in sight, eat whatever strikes his fancy,
and has the best laugh.

Acknowledgments

Thank you to Greg and Cade Radenbaugh. I had a hard time finding a model for this cover. I wanted authenticity and sometimes that is hard to find when it comes to outdoorsy, hunting-oriented images... especially for romance covers. So my husband had the genius idea of asking a friend, and Cade came through for me. He and his dad, Greg, sent me the perfect shot of Cade to use as Seth Hastings. And I'm so thankful! Authentic, legit, genuine, and real... this is Seth Hastings! Thank you, Cade for agreeing to be on the cover for me.

Author and writer friends are gems. Thank you to Susan Faw for helping me knock out some words with writing sprints and encouragement.

Thank you to Erin Davis for teaching me key information about the oil industry, and for the writing sprints, "table-talk", and pep talks.

Thank you to my editor, Lauren Hanson.

Thank you to my cover designer, Kerry Prater.

And thank you to my beta readers and my readers all across the world. You guys keep me encouraged and blown away by your support.

H

Chapter One

He felt like a spy. Not 007 spy, in a clean suit and with beautiful women hanging on his arm, but the kind of spy that traveled to foreign countries and trekked through the wilderness to capture pictures of a criminal mastermind. Only, instead of wilderness, he was on the ranch. And by criminal mastermind, he meant elk. Seth Hastings and his brother Clint had been tracking this particular elk herd since the previous year, and like all good things, they had to wait for the elk to make their appearance on their terms. If that meant sitting in a pop-up blind before sunrise on a cool morning, then that's what had to be done. The weather didn't bother Seth. In fact, he found the cooler months refreshing after the miserably hot and long summers they had in west Texas. He just added the necessary layer of clothing, which he'd shed by noon, grabbed his binoculars, a snack, and he was set for hours of sitting. Sometimes he'd bring a book to look at, but the elk were something he couldn't miss by being wrapped up in the latest thriller he'd borrowed from Ruby. He'd never hear the end of it from his brothers.

"Oh, Seth was in la la land again."

"Can't focus on one thing at a time."

"Scatter-brained Seth."

Or the worst one:

"Stop being undependable."

He didn't get the last one much, but when he did it was like a bullet to the heart. He worked hard on the 7H. Thanks to Graham and his older brothers, with the help of Annie and Henry, he'd grown up on the family land. As the youngest brother, and the one with the fewest memories of their parents, God rest their souls, Seth valued his oldest brother's opinion of him. Graham sacrificed a lot to keep the family ranch moving forward. He also bore the responsibility of six younger brothers over the years, and though Graham was a tough cookie most days, he was more of a father to Seth than their actual dad. Seth was grateful to him. And glad that Graham had found the beautiful Julia to say 'I do' to and have the opportunity to start a family of his own. He could tell Graham was a bit nervous about the prospect, but Seth had no doubts that he'd do just fine. He'd already done it, really.

He took an overly sized mouthful of his granola bar and chomped, his eyes narrowing on the brush line. He raised his binos a moment to check the movement. Not much wind, so a critter of some kind rattled the foliage. A wild hog ventured out, sniffing the ground, followed by one, two, three... twelve baby piglets. Seth sighed. Wild hogs were cute, but they were nuisances. And mean. He hated hogs. They tore up pastures with their rooting around, they disturbed the troughs, ate the corn from the feeders... just nuisances. And if the elk, as skittish as they'd been, avoid their usual watering grounds because of the stinkin' hog and piglets, Seth *and* Clint would be aggravated.

Last year, the elk were completely off limits. They didn't cross over to the 7H enough to warrant a serious effort in maintenance or hunting. But over the last year, they'd noticed more and more that the elk were venturing from the neighboring ranch, Chandler's Crossing, over to the 7H and farther into the interior. It was just a matter of tracking consistency. Where did they hole up most of the time? Where were they at this time of day or that? How many bulls were there? The typical surveillance needed to gauge whether or not a hunting opportunity could be scheduled.

They hoped to have a few elk hunting packages sold this year, but time was slowly slipping away. The rut was happening soon, for typically between September and October, but this crew of elk had been dragging their feet. He hadn't seen any signs of rut, even with the cold snap that had blown through. And yet, he sat. And he sat until the sun brightened the sky and the morning dew began to sweat. Exhaling a defeated breath, he watched as the hog and her piglets meandered back into the brush. He fished out his cell phone and sent a text to Clint letting him know there was no action on his end, and he was packing it up. He packed his backpack with his gear and stepped out of the camouflaged hiding spot completely immersed in its surroundings. He stretched his back, the hours of sitting making his muscles tight, and then began his walk back towards the dirt road that would lead to his truck. He'd need to check the garden today. That was one of his main responsibilities on the ranch. He'd grown up in the garden with Annie. She'd taught him everything she knew, and with Annie, that meant *a lot*. And gardening in west Texas wasn't easy due to the heat levels they hit in the summer. But Seth knew what worked and what didn't, how to shade some areas of the garden, how to plant his summer squashes in the full sun, how to keep at least a little dappled sun and shade on the tomatoes, no matter what the seed packet said, and he knew that no matter what the conditions, he could always grow jalapeno peppers. Lately, he'd been clearing out the plants that had seen their time come to an end and refreshing the soil for a fall garden planting. He liked mapping out the rows. No one really challenged him on what vegetables he grew. Not even Graham. All they cared about was the provision. As long as the garden made, they didn't care what they ate. He liked that. He liked that he could contribute something useful and necessary to the ranch. Sure, he helped in all areas wherever he was needed, but the garden was his. Annie didn't even venture through it much anymore. She'd walk the rows once a season to check his layout, growth, and plant inventory, but that was mostly so she could gauge what to cook for supper when she decided to spoil them.

Now, however, Julia handled most of the spoiling on the ranch when it came to filling stomachs. The woman could cook, and he didn't bring it up for the sake of liking his nose where it sat, but he'd noticed Graham had stored away a couple of extra pounds since Julia had started cooking for him every evening. Seth smirked at that thought as he reached his truck. He opened the door quietly so that if he'd overlooked any other wildlife in the area, he wouldn't disturb or scare them away from the path. And with his mind on Julia's cookin', he directed his truck towards Graham's house. Breakfast was in order.

~

Charlotte despised early mornings. Though she'd been living on her grandpa's ranch for the last two months, she still wasn't used to waking up before dawn to start her day. Granted, she'd spent the last three years working the night shift at Baylor Medical. Typically, when the wee hours of the morning rolled around, Charlotte, or Charlie, as she liked to be called, was ending her day. She'd shuffle her way to her car, slip inside, yawn, head to her efficiency apartment, and crash for several hours before waking around noon or one in the afternoon and taking care of daylight hour tasks like grocery shopping and checking the mail. Otherwise, Charlotte was a lady of the night, in a purely non-scandalous sort of way. She worked the emergency room as a registered nurse, and from the moment she walked into work, she was on her feet rushing around until it was time for her to go home. *If* she actually even went home. She'd slept in the breakroom a time or two depending on the hospital's needs. She loved her job. She loved helping people. She also loved her stubborn, grumpy, rude, and sometimes downright mean grandpa. And whether or not she liked the idea of uprooting herself and moving to a new place, she recognized a need when she saw it. And her grandpa needed her.

Her mom and dad, aunts, uncles, and cousins were scattered around the country. And though her parents were only a half a day's drive away from Parks, Texas, her dad did not have one bone in his body that embraced the ranch lifestyle he'd grown up with. Craven Chandler bucked the system. As the oldest son and immediate heir to the Chandler Crossing Ranch, he had opted for life in the city over a west Texas ranch. His younger sister, CeeCee, married well, but moved to the east coast— Myrtle Beach to be exact— and had no desire to take on the responsibility of the family ranch. Her children didn't care much about the ranch either, except when they wanted to schedule a hunt for themselves or for their various company retreats. That left Charlotte.

She'd loved coming to the ranch as a kid. She loved her gruff and hard grandpa, who really, deep down, just needed a big hug and some loving. He was a hard man, but after her grandmother passed away nearly fifteen years ago, he'd only grown even more sour. She couldn't blame him. She couldn't imagine losing the love of your life and then living so remotely by yourself. But Bob Chandler had turned mean somewhere along the way. Not to her, really, but to everyone around him. His family, friends, and even his neighbors. If she had a dime for every time he'd complained about the Hastings family, she'd be able to buy her own private island outright. His hatred ran deep. And out of her own curiosity, when the invitation came to the oldest Hastings brother's wedding, she'd accepted and went. No one knew her. No one cared who she was even when they met her. Everyone was genuinely happy another person had come to celebrate Graham and his new bride. She liked that. She even enjoyed the few small conversations sprinkled throughout the night. And when she left, she couldn't quite understand her grandpa's issue with the Hastings crew.

But, no matter how hard she tried to talk sense into him about 'loving thy neighbor,' Grandpa wasn't hearing her. His prejudice towards the brothers ran too deep, and this not only affected his relationship with his neighbors but also the townspeople. The Hastings family was well-respected, their ranch renowned, anyone who openly disdained them was a conundrum, and not in a good way. Her grandpa had lost work crews, ranch hands, and contractors over his prejudice. If he found out any of the above had stepped foot on the 7H prior to his place, he'd immediately fire them for disloyalty. Well, that didn't bode well for Chandler's Crossing. The ranch had suffered from lack of attention. Not enough hands to spread the work around. Now the ranch was overgrown, brush invaded, overgrazed, and lacking. It broke her heart to see it in such a state. That, too, was one of the reasons she'd moved to Parks. If the ranch was to remain in the family and she was the only family member willing to take care of it, then so be it. If her grandpa needed medical attention, but was too stubborn to get it, then so be it. She'd see to both. She'd help both. She wasn't sure how, but she would. She'd learn what needed to be done to get the ranch back in operation, how it used to be. Chandler's Crossing needed help, and Charlie was bound and determined to mend what she could. And if she had to talk to a Hastings or two to make that happen, then so be it.

H

Chapter Two

"*Seth, honey, fetch two* packages of those rolls there, please." Annie pointed up the aisle of the grocery store and Seth obediently trekked towards the rows of bread.

"I'm surprised you're buyin' rolls, Annie." He reached for a bag, and she shook her head, pointing to the one next to it. He grabbed two packages and brought them to her shopping cart. "You normally make your rolls."

"Time is of the essence, Seth." Annie glanced down at her list penned onto a small red pocket notebook she used *only* for her grocery trips. "If I'm to have everything ready for tomorrow after church, I can't waste time waiting for dough to rise."

"I bet Julia would help if you asked her."

"Honey, she does not need to be on her feet so much this late in her pregnancy. She also doesn't need to be liftin' and bendin' over. She needs to take it easy. She already pushes herself too much." Annie motioned for them to head down the next aisle, Seth dodging a bypassing cart. He'd agreed to help Annie with her shopping in Sheffield for the day; though Annie refused to admit it, she needed help too when it came to lifting. The brothers now sent one of their number to help her on grocery and errand runs, so as to prevent her from hurting herself or overdoing it.

"Well, I bet Ruby'd hook us up with some rolls from the diner."

Annie crossed her arms, her narrow hip tilting in what could only be described as her 'I'm suspicious of you' way. "Is this you balkin' at the idea of eatin' a store-bought roll, honey?"

Seth smirked. "I'm spoiled, what can I say?"

She dropped her arms and gave him a motherly pat as she went back to pushing her cart. "You are. And it's my own fault. But I love ya any way, and because I love you, I'm going to tell you that you're goin' to eat these store-bought rolls and you're goin' to love them. And if you don't, you act like you do or I'll box your ears into next week. Now, let me check my list."

Seth grabbed a box of snack crackers off the shelf, reading the label, a young woman in her early twenties settled beside him, her eyes roaming over all the cracker options. She gave a frustrated sigh. "So, what do you do if the one cracker they want isn't on the shelf?" she wondered aloud.

Seth turned to offer a friendly smile and pulled back a touch. He recognized the woman. Though she had her hair tied back in a perky ponytail of choppy blonde hair and wore a simple plain t-shirt and jeans, Seth remembered that face. The blue eyes, the tidy lips that were painted a bold red. Only today, they weren't red. They were plain, void of makeup. But he remembered Charlotte Chandler from Graham's wedding. Clearly, she didn't remember him.

"Well, what cracker are you after?"

"Oh, the bland wheat ones that taste like you're eating a sticker burr."

He laughed and she looked up at him with a small grin.

"Well, I apologize then, because I can't pinpoint which one to suggest to you. I'm pretty sure this entire shelf would be better than a sticker burr."

"Very true." Her eyes washed over the cracker options once more and she reached out for a box, her hand hesitant before she dropped it by her side again on an annoyed sigh. "I may have to go to another store and see if they have them. Heaven forbid I buy the wrong one."

"They might just be out of them. There's no other option for you as far as stores go. Maybe ask if they have some in the back?"

"Oh." Disappointment fell over her pretty features. "I guess you're right. That's a good idea. Thanks." She looked up at him and gave a polite smile.

"Seth, would you come on!" Annie waved for him at the end of the aisle and paused, her face lifting into a bright smile. "Well, well, well... you're Charlotte, are you not?"

The young woman's brows knit together as she tried to process if she knew the older woman before her.

"Annie. We met at Graham Hastings' wedding this past spring. You're Bob Chandler's granddaughter, isn't that right?"

"Oh, yes ma'am. Good to see you again."

"You too, honey. You livin' on the ranch these days?"

"I am, yes. I haven't been out there but a couple of months now."

"Well, bless your heart." Annie patted her shoulder. "How's that stick in the mud grandpa of yours?"

"Annie..." Seth hissed a warning and Charlotte laughed as Annie waved his concern away.

"Seems you know him well."

"I know *of* him. Bob Chandler refuses to let anyone actually *know* him," Annie corrected.

"Well, other than trying to fulfill his impossible grocery list, he keeps me on my toes and seems to enjoy that, so I guess you could say he is doing okay."

Annie tilted Charlotte's list down and perused it. "Oh, crackers, that's what you're lookin' for?" She fished in her own cart and pulled up a box of the crackers Charlotte needed. "Take this box. Lord knows I don't want them at my house."

"Then why are they in your cart, Annie?" Seth asked.

"Because Henry loves them. Don't ask my why. To me, it's like eatin' hay. He might as well join the cows on the hay ring if he likes these dried sticks."

Seth lightly laughed and extended his hand. "Seth Hastings. I think we met briefly at the wedding, but don't think we had a chance to really speak to one another."

Charlotte shook his hand. "Charlie Chandler, nice to meet you."

"Charlie, hm?" His lips tilted. "I like it."

Tealizing she was lingering too long, Charlie shouldered her purse. "Well, thank you for the crackers. You saved me a future headache."

"Oh, no problem, honey." Annie gave her shoulder an encouraging pat. "Any time. You don't be a stranger now, okay? You living that far out and secluded, it's important you meet your neighbors." She eyed Seth. "It can get lonely out on those ranches if you don't have anyone to talk to."

"Of course." Charlie ducked her head, knowing that her even conversing with a Hastings in the grocery store would be frowned upon by her grandpa, much less conversing across the property line. "Thank you, again." She tucked the crackers in her basket and scurried off.

"A pretty one, that one," Seth admitted. "It's a shame she's a Chandler."

Annie swatted his arm and he jumped at the force behind the blow. "Just because she is does not mean you can't be nice to her. Just because her grandpa and your daddy and grandpa had fits doesn't mean you have to. That poor girl will need some company out there or she's going to go crazy. We'll have to sic the girls on her."

"The girls?"

"Yes, the girls." Annie looked up at him as if he were stupid. "Julia, Alice, Helena, Ruby, Ali, and Bailey... the girls. Women need other women, Seth. It's a fact. You best learn it."

"Yes ma'am. Though if ol' Chandler hates Hastings men, then I doubt he'll appreciate the women that love them either."

"It's not about him," Annie added. "It's about her. I don't care what Bob Chandler thinks. Never have. He's an old recluse who has more enemies battling it out inside his head than he does actually around him. But his sour attitude has led to him living on that ranch by himself, miserable and lonely. I don't want that to suck his sweet granddaughter down a rabbit hole of despair."

"Have you ever thought she might like it out there? I mean, she moved out there." Seth pointed out.

"No one likes being lonely." Annie pointed her finger in his chest. "Just ask your brothers. I doubt any of them would go back to the lives they had before their girls swept them off their feet. Not a one."

"Well, I'm not lonely," Seth added.

"Because you're spoiled. You're surrounded by your brothers and their women, and you're doted on because we all love you. You don't have a chance to be lonely."

"And I'm grateful." Seth grinned. "But not when I have to eat store-bought rolls." He pulled a face to make her laugh and loved when her familiar cackle rang out in the store.

"Get on with you now. Let's finish this list and get home, or the only grumpy man I will be dealin' with is Henry." Zipping through the rows of the store to complete her long list of supplies, Seth was grateful when he loaded the last bag of groceries into her trunk and shut the door. As Annie settled in her seat, he walked the cart back towards the store to return it to the long line stacked up outside.

He watched as an empty cart rolled across the parking lot and paused a moment as it wheeled directly towards an unaware Charlie Chandler as she put her own grocery bags in her car. He nudged his cart aside and sprinted forward.

Charlie glanced up at the sound of his boots beating against the pavement and her eyes widened at him running straight towards her. She raised her hands to block her face as if he were running up to attack her, but he pulled up just shy of running straight into her, his arm reaching around her and gripping the metal rim of the rogue shopping cart that had almost slammed into her back. Breathless, he stepped to the side to wheel the cart around her to face it the direction of his own. "It almost got ya."

She placed a hand over her heart. "Wow, thank you. I—"

He tipped his cowboy hat. "Have a good day, Ms. Chandler." He retrieved his own cart and wheeled both towards the store and he could see and feel her watchful blue eyes following his every step.

~

She shifted the can of beans to the right, stacked it with the other cans of various beans she'd found at the back of the pantry, and then placed the two new cans of green beans beside them, because she bought them thinking they were out of beans. She placed a hand to her forehead and bit back an annoyed growl as she checked the date on a can of cream of mushroom soup that had a nice collection of dust on top. Clearly her grandpa didn't inventory his food supply much as the soup was three years out of date. She heard him shuffling across the terrazzo tile towards the kitchen. His broad shoulders filled the doorway and he watched as she tossed the soup can towards the trash can and it landed with a hard thud.

"Not right to throw food out. I don't like to waste."

"Well, if it wasn't old, then I wouldn't have to throw it away, Grandpa. Seriously, when was the last time you checked these cabinets?"

"Been awhile."

"I can tell." She watched as he picked up the box of crackers she'd just bought and set it on the island countertop. "I like the ones with cracked black pepper."

"They were out. Those were the only ones I could find, and even that one came from someone else's cart."

His brows lifted. "You stole them out of someone's buggy?"

"No." She walked towards the island and began pulling out other items she needed to put away. "A nice woman offered them to me when she realized they were what I was looking for and it was the last box."

"Awfully nice."

"I thought so." Charlie walked back towards the pantry. "Was there something you needed? Need a sandwich or something?"

"No. No food. Just came to see when you'd like to sit down and map out next week's work plan."

"I can tackle that after this. I want to put some supper on in the slow cooker first though. So maybe in about thirty minutes?"

"Alright." He sat at the small dinette table and sipped on his mug of cold coffee left there from breakfast.

"Was there anything else?" Charlie asked.

"No." His gruff, no-nonsense reply had her briefly closing her eyes and taking a deep breath before ignoring him and going about the tasks before her.

After she plopped the porkchops into the slow cooker, covering them with a non-out of date can of cream of mushroom soup and a seasoning packet, she turned the knob to set the temperature and walked towards the table. Sitting opposite him and grabbing a notebook and pen, she said. "Okay, go."

"We need to work the cows."

"Alright. Do we need any supplies for that?"

"No, I've got it. We just need some hands."

"What about Rance?"

"He quit."

Disappointed, she leaned back in her chair. "When?"

"This mornin'."

"Why?"

"Doesn't matter." He narrowed his eyes at her and pointed to her notebook. "He was no good anyway."

"That's not true," she pointed out. "But I'll let your opinion slide if you tell me you have somewhere we can find more ranch hands at this short of notice."

"Check with the feedstore. There's sometimes men who list their info on a sheet on the community board there."

"Alright. And if not?"

"Start there. That will be enough."

"But what if there are no men looking for work?"

"There will be."

"But what if there isn't?" she challenged again.

He slapped a hand on the table, and she jumped. "Just do what I asked."

"Alright, fine. I will go by the feed store and see what my options are. Just need them for cattle work?"

"They need to be good on a horse too, because we gotta gather up the cattle and condense them down to one pasture for the winter."

"Okay, so before we can work the cows, we need to find them. Got it."

"No need findin' them. I know where they're at. We just need to clean out the pastures and move them to where they need to be."

"So how many men am I looking at here?"

"As many as we can get this time of year."

Sighing, she penciled that note down. "I'll go by there on Monday and see who I can find. I thought about going to church tomorrow in town. Would you like to go?"

"No." He pushed back from the table and stood, his signal that their conversation was ending.

"And what about today?" she asked.

"Make yourself useful. It's a ranch, there's always something that needs to be done," he called over his shoulder as she watched him walk out the front door, pulling his worn cowboy hat down over his thick white hair.

She prayed for patience. She prayed for her sanity. She also prayed that she wouldn't beat him over the head with a can of beans for being so cold all the time. But that's why she was here, she reminded herself. They were family. He'd been happy once. Loving. It was only a matter of time before maybe, just maybe, she could help him be that way again. In the meantime, like he'd so kindly pointed out, there was work that needed to be done. And Charlie had learned over the last couple of months that when she needed a breath of fresh air and to feel productive, she'd work on clearing out the brambles and weeds that had invaded the side of the house and the garden her grandmother used to plant. She'd been working on it the entire time she'd been at the ranch. It was her goal to have the entire plot cleaned up, tilled, and ready for planting come spring. But she had her work cut out for her. Fifteen years of growth and neglect had made that section of the yard unrecognizable. And though she caught her grandpa snarling over the project several times, it was important to her. The garden was one of her best memories of the ranch. She'd walk the rows with her grandma and spend all day amongst the plants and the scents and the woman that radiated warmth like the sun. Charlie needed that feeling now, especially now that she lived on the ranch. It was no longer a bright and cheerful place with rolling green pastures, deep ravines, and beautiful cattle and wildlife scattered around. It was overgrown, rough, tough, and ugly. And so was the man running it. It broke her heart to see him and the land in such a state.

She didn't know everything there was to know about ranching; it would be an enormous learning curve for her. But she was determined. She wanted to revive the place. If she was to make a life here, she *needed* to revive the place or she wouldn't make it. Life needed to seep into the very roots of the ranch for her and it to continue on. If she couldn't take on the task of running the ranch, or prove to her grandpa that she could, then Chandler's Crossing was at a loss.

H

Chapter Three

Seth loved Sundays. Not only was the day a restful one from work, but he loved having lunch after church at Annie and Henry's house. He wasn't sure when the tradition started. For as far back as he could remember, they came to Annie's after church to be filled up not only on food, but love and attention from the older couple. He loved that the long wooden picnic table in the backyard was now made longer by adding two additional tables to house all the new additions to his brothers' lives. He loved that Annie and Henry's shaded backyard offered an oasis from the Texas heat, even during their scorching summers, that each week, no matter the heat index, they could enjoy a lunch around the table outside. It was rare that anyone missed a Sunday lunch. In fact, up until Graham's honeymoon with Julia, he wasn't sure his oldest brother had ever missed one.

"Do I have something on my face?" Graham asked, feeling Seth's scrutiny and not liking the extra attention.

"What?" Seth asked.

"You're staring at me."

"Maybe you're just nice to look at." Julia leaned over and kissed Graham's cheek as his brothers laughed at the light flush that stained Graham's face from her comment.

"No, I was just thinkin'."

"About what?" Graham asked.

"About how I don't think you've ever missed a Sunday lunch at Annie's, really."

"Okay..." Graham looked confused as to why that would even be on Seth's mind.

"I was just tryin' to think how long we'd been doing this is all."

"Too long and not long enough." Henry's open smile had Annie lightly patting his hand before removing the extra roll he'd laid on his plate. He briefly frowned before reaching for an extra deviled egg to replace it.

"It's true," Lawrence said, reaching over and briefly squeezing Ruby's knee next to him said, "I think we've all been coming here since our teens. I, for one, am grateful." Echoes of the same sentiment traveled around the table.

"It warms my heart that we've had to expand the last year or so." Annie nudged Alejandra next to her, pleased that Hayes' girlfriend and her daughter were part of that expansion. "I just love having some female presence these days. I just don't think I can get enough." Annie beamed at all the women.

"I'd get tired of these boys too, Annie." Alice Wilkenson, the local vet, family friend, and now Calvin's girlfriend, grinned as she popped a bite of a roll into her mouth and smirked at Clint across the table. "Though we're missing one of the amazing women that we've grown to love. Where's Bailey at, Clint? She already wise up and boot you to the curb?"

"No, Doc, she's still wrapped around my finger." He winked and leaned back in his usual arrogance with his arms crossed over his chest. "She's workin'. Unlike you, she can't take all her weekends off."

"I don't ta—"

Calvin reached over and rested a cooling hand on Alice's.

"Right. Well," Alice continued. "I'm glad to hear she hasn't left the picture. I like her. And if you screw it up, I'll kick your b—"

"Not at the table, Al." Lawrence shook his head in dismay. "Can't I just enjoy my meal without you and Clint goin' at each other's throats? Besides, you should be mad at Hayes."

"Me?" Hayes, upon hearing the slander to his name, turned his attention to the conversation.

"Yeah." Lawrence waved his hand towards his brother. "You're the one that was talkin' about having Al come out to the stables later today and doing full checkups on your horses... on her day off."

"Is that so?" Alice asked, her eyes narrowed in challenge upon Hayes.

"It was a thought." He held up a finger to ward off her upcoming tangent. "But I didn't ask, because my sweethearts came to see me." He winked at Ava, Alejandra's little girl. "And my afternoon is already booked."

As if disappointed there wasn't at least one argument to battle across the table, Lawrence went back to eating in defeat.

"Julia, when's your next doctor's appointment?" Annie asked.

Julia lightly rested a hand on her oversized belly, a glow of pure pleasure radiating across her face as she said, "Wednesday. And I think we might actually get to see the baby."

"You still aren't finding out what it is?" Seth asked.

"Nope. We want it to be a surprise."

"*She* wants it to be a surprise," Graham corrected his wife. "I want to find out."

"I still think it's a girl." Clint held up his hand as if to tally his vote.

"Me too," Ruby agreed.

"No way." Phillip shook his head. "There's no way Graham would have a girl."

"Well, since it's Julia doin' the havin'," Annie interjected. "I'm going with girl also."

"That's just because you want a baby girl to spoil," Calvin pointed out.

"You betcha. Can't have enough of these little gals runnin' around." Annie lightly tugged on Ava's ponytail as she placed a small plate of angel food cake in front of the little girl for dessert.

"What about you, Julia? What are you feeling?" Helena, Phillip's girlfriend, leaned forward to look at her friend up the table.

"Feeling? As if that has anything to do with it." Lawrence chuckled and shook his head as Ruby lightly squeezed his hand.

Julia inhaled a deep breath and gently reached for Graham's hand to hold it. "I don't know. There are days I feel like it's a boy. And then I'll have a dream and wake up thinking it's a girl. Either way, I can't wait to find out. And I definitely can't wait to not have swollen ankles anymore."

"Bless your heart." Annie nodded towards Ali, "You do what Ali suggested? You puttin' your feet up throughout the day?"

"I am," Julia reported. "Even if Alice gets annoyed."

"I don't get annoyed," Alice defended before crumbling under Julia's doubtful look. "All the time," she amended. "It's just taking me time to get used to Julia not buzzing around everywhere. I'm getting there, though."

"That you are," Julia encouraged.

"Guess the sermon preacher spoke today about being kind to one another and tender hearted was aimed at you, Al." Seth grinned.

"Not just me... though maybe a little."

"It's always good to listen to the sermon and internalize its message," Henry explained. "That's how we grow."

"And speakin' of being kind to others," Seth forked an extra piece of ham onto his plate before continuing. "Did y'all see old man Chandler's granddaughter sittin' towards the back of the church?"

"Charlotte?" Annie asked.

He nodded. "Yep. I saw her sneakin' out before the preacher even made it back there to shake hands."

"Well, I'll be." Annie, disappointed, shook her head. "I would have loved to have said hello to her. Good on her for comin' to church. I bet her grandpa didn't like that one bit."

"Best if we just steer clear of any Chandlers," Clint suggested. "He made it very clear to me last year he didn't want to talk or look at a Hastings."

"Well, you're ugly. I don't blame him." Alice grinned at her success of fitting in another insult at Clint.

"Man, Al... give it up." Clint rolled his eyes. "All I'm saying is that when I called him about the elk, he lied to me, and Bailey said he warned her not to deal with us."

"That poor girl is going to need some company." Annie looked to all the men around the table. "It may not be you boys, but we have some pretty incredible women seated at this table that might could reach out and see if Charlie needs anything."

"I'll do it," Julia said. "I could make a dinner and take it over to her."

"Honey—" Annie started, but Julia interrupted.

"I can make a casserole, Annie. It won't be too much for me, I promise."

"Well, make Seth take you over there when you're ready to do it."

"Why Seth?" Lawrence asked.

"Because Charlie has met him before and they chatted quite nicely. He'd be a familiar face. And, if her grandpa happens to be at home when Julia goes to knockin', he won't shoot Graham dead if he isn't there."

Graham harumphed at the truth to her statement, though he found no humor in it.

"He's about to be a daddy, I doubt even Bob Chandler would shoot him down now," Phillip suggested.

"Don't put it past him," Graham muttered.

"You just let me know when, Jewels." Seth nodded his sister-in-law's direction and she smiled warmly.

"Now that that is settled," Lawrence stood and clapped his hands together. "Who's up for dessert?"

~

Charlie brushed a dirty glove over her forehead as she nudged her loose bangs out of the way. She'd been tugging on the random root ball of whatever small tree had once graced the corner of the garden for at least ten minutes and all she managed was a slight shifting in the roots. Unless she packed on another twenty pounds of muscle in the next five minutes, it wasn't moving without the help of a piece of equipment. Frustrated, she climbed to her feet and brushed off the knees of her jeans at the sound of tires crunching over gravel and saw a blue pickup drove up the drive towards the house. She didn't recognize the vehicle, and she watched as her grandpa stepped out of the house and onto the front porch to see who the visitor was. They rarely received visitors. In fact, most sane people steered clear of Chandler's Crossing.

A woman past the midway mark in pregnancy slowly slid out of the passenger side of the truck. She was beautiful, with her dark hair pulled back in a styled ponytail, and a cute maternity top that made her look as if she modeled the clothing for a high-end retailer. Out of the other side of the truck, a man slipped out, sliding his cowboy hat on his head at the same time and her stomach dropped. Seth Hastings. Her eyes quickly darted to her grandpa, and she hurried to the porch steps as the woman, who she now recognized as the bride and wife of Graham Hastings, walked confidently towards him carrying a glass covered dish.

"Hi there," Julia greeted. "I'm Julia Hastings." She extended her hand to Bob, and he eyed it suspiciously before shaking it, his eyes never leaving Seth's face. "We happened to see your granddaughter, Charlotte, at church yesterday. Her eyes shifted to an approaching Charlie and her smile bloomed even further. "Charlotte, hi. I'm Julia." Charlotte pulled her glove off her hand and embraced Julia's in a friendly shake. "I'm so glad to meet you. Seth and Annie said they'd bumped into you at the grocery store and Seth saw you at church yesterday," Julia continued, Charlie shooting a gaze towards the youngest Hastings brother, discretely standing away from their interaction and close to his truck so as not to upset the balance of things. He gave her a polite nod, his eyes shaded by his hat. "Anyway, it's nice to hear of another woman moving this far out of town, and I wanted to bring you guys a meal and introduce myself." Julia handed the dish over to Bob without qualms, the old man fumbling with it as if not expecting to be the recipient. "Also, Mr. Chandler, I have yet to meet you as well. We missed you at the wedding."

Burn, thought Charlie, looking to her grandpa to see how he handled that comment. He stared at the woman before him as if she were a completely new species.

"I told Graham it's important for me to meet the neighbors and what not. I'm not from around here and this lifestyle is completely new to me. And I'm sorry I haven't made it over sooner, but..." She held her hands to her rotund belly. "I've been a bit preoccupied." She smiled and then turned her attention back to Charlie. "Some friends and I get together on Wednesday evenings at my house to eat and chat, sometimes play cards. I'd love if you joined us."

Stunned at the invite, Charlie muttered a quiet, "Thank you."

"We appreciate the meal, Mrs. Hastings," Bob began, his hands already extending to return it to Julia. "But we're fine."

She waved away his return. "Oh no. That's for you guys. You can eat it, burn it, toss it to the chickens... but it's yours." She flashed a forced but polite smile, her eyes challenging Bob, and Charlie bit back a grin of her own as her grandpa tried to maneuver a way of mistreating such a friendly person. "Besides, I'm technically not supposed to be up on my feet. Doctor's orders. And I spent most of the afternoon putting that together. I'd hate to see it go to waste." Nodding towards Charlie, she reminded her, "Wednesdays at six, if you can make it. It was a pleasure." Julia stepped down off the porch and nodded towards Seth and he opened her truck door and gave a helping hand to help her inside the vehicle. Bob Chandler walked back into his house, casserole in hand, the screen door slamming behind him. Charlie stood on the porch a moment, offering a wave before walking back to the garden area and bracing for the tug of war with the root ball. She turned, sensing a presence and gawked as Seth Hastings stood next to her. "Got yourself a good spot for a garden here."

"That's the plan," she whispered, her eyes darting towards the house.

"Need help with that root?"

"W-what are you doing?" she asked. "If my grandpa comes back out—"

"Then he'll face off with Jewels again. She's the one that spotted this root ball here. Said she bet you were tryin' to pull and dig it out. She insisted I help you before we left."

"Oh." Charlie turned to cast a glance towards the truck and Julia waved with a friendly smile. "Is she always so nice?"

Seth beamed in pride. "Yep. Hard to imagine, I know. Especially being married to Graham. But she's a little sunbeam, and mighty hard to disappoint. Can I give you a hand?" He pointed to the root ball again and she nodded. With a couple of hard tugs, it was free, and he tossed it aside. "That ought to do it."

"Thank you. I've been working on that thing for way longer than I intended."

"No problem. Gardening is sort of my specialty, and digging up and pulling out invasive plants, weeds, and roots is one of the few things I can handle." He winked. "Take care, Ms. Charlotte."

"Charlie," she reminded him.

"Right. Charlie. I'll remember." He tapped his temple.

"And thank you." She motioned towards Julia. "For the food and for saving me at the grocery store from the runaway cart. Not sure I properly thanked you for that." She slid her hands into her back pockets as she spoke, and noticed his head tilted towards the house as the front door opened once again and her grandpa stepped outside. "You better go."

Seth's eyes held her grandpa's as he tapped the brim of his hat in farewell and hopped into his truck. Seconds later, they were gone.

"What did that Hastings boy want?" Bob asked.

"He helped me with the root." She pointed to the discard pile, and he crossed his arms over his burly chest. "You need help, you ask me." And with that, he stormed back inside.

H

Chapter Four

Seth leaned against the counter at Phillip's feed store and waited for Phillip to come out from the back storage part of the store with his order. "So," Phillip handed him the small paper sacks holding the various vegetable seeds he needed for fall planting in the garden. "Mr. Chandler didn't say anything to you being there?"

"Nope. Julia tamed him like a snake with a flute… or whatever those things are that snake charmers use." Seth chuckled. "She didn't really give him a minute to buck back. Now I see how she and Graham must get along."

Phillip grinned and his face sobered as his eyes looked beyond the windows of his store and Charlotte Chandler reached for the door to walk inside. "Best keep our conversation quiet now," he warned as she looked towards them upon entering. Surprise lit her gaze at seeing Seth. "Two times in one day, Ms. Charlie. I'm beginning to think we should be friends."

Her lips gave a brief and polite smile as she looked to Phillip. "Hi. I'm looking for the 'community board' that might have a listing of some hands looking for work. I was told it was here at the feed store."

"I can point you that direction." Phillip flipped up the counter door and stepped out and pointed to a far wall that had an overly papered bulletin board nailed to the wall above a pegboard that housed various metal chain lengths and widths. "Not much on there right now as most hands are booked up for the upcoming season, but you might find one or two tucked in somewhere." He pointed to a ratty business card and tugged it off the board. "I'll just do you a favor on this one and throw it in the trash." He ripped the card. "Last person who hired him mysteriously lost an electric drill and a handsaw."

"Thanks." Her eyes perused the board.

"May I ask what type of work you're needing done?"

"Mostly working cows and some horseback work."

"Ah. A little late to be workin' cows, isn't it?" Seth asked, walking over.

"A bit," she agreed. "I don't see any cards or notes or papers of any people on here willing to work. All of these are advertisements."

"Yeah, I told ya," Phillip stated. "It's pretty slim this time of year."

"Is there anywhere else I could go to find help?"

"You could reach out to some neighboring ranches. Maybe they have some men to spare for a few days. Unless you're looking for hands to last you for the season," Phillip suggested.

She shook her head. "Not that I know of. I think really we're just looking for some guys to come in and clean out the pasture, consolidate the herd, work the cows, and that's it."

"Easy enough." Seth slapped Phillip on the back. "Sign us up."

Phillip chuckled. "Easy, bro. Need I remind you, I don't do horses?"

"Oh, right. Well, the rest of us do. We'll help you, Ms. Charlie." He paused as they stared at him. "What?"

"I— well— I—" Charlie's cheeks warmed.

"I think what she's trying to politely say, Seth, is that she and her grandpa aren't desperate enough to seek our help." Phillip held up a hand in peace when she started to negate his comment. "Don't worry, ma'am. We don't take offense."

"Well, I do." Seth crossed his arms. "Ol' Chandler needs help, he shouldn't care where it comes from. And we're the best at what he's needing. I'll talk to Graham."

"Seth," Phillip shook his head. "It's not that simple, and Graham is going to say no." He turned towards Charlie. "Respectfully, of course."

"No, I understand what you're saying. I'd love to have the help, but my grandpa really dislikes your family. Like... really hates you guys." She grimaced, "I don't know if he will go for it."

"Then don't tell him. We'll just show up and do it." Seth held up his hands, curious as to why they didn't think his plan was a good one. It made sense to him. Someone needed help, they could help them, so prejudices needed to be pushed aside. Simple.

"I appreciate you being willing to help." Charlie looked at both the brothers, liking the sympathetic understanding from Phillip and the eager willingness of Seth. "If only things were different, right?"

"How are they to change if no one changes them?" Seth countered, and had both Phillip and Charlie equally impressed with his quick clapback. "You taking over Chandler's Crossing?"

"Well… not yet. Fully. But eventually that is the plan. Potentially. We'll see," she trailed off. "I have a lot to learn. I'm a nurse, not a ranch hand, so I'm afraid I don't know the ins and outs yet. And my grandpa isn't the most willing teacher right now, but maybe soon." She gave a hopeful but forced shoulder shrug and smile. "Thanks for your help. Can you let me know if anyone comes in looking for work?"

Phillip nodded.

Seth reached for her arm and lightly tugged on her soft sleeved sweater. "Wait. Come on now, Charlie, let us do this. You're not going to find help this late in the year. And not just because people are busy, but because nobody, and I mean, nobody, wants to work for Bob Chandler."

Phillip groaned that his brother let slip that piece of information.

"And why is that?" she asked.

"Have you met your grandpa?" Seth chuckled. "He runs off anyone he hires. It's no secret, and I'm not going to pretend that you can just find help from the community board and be on your way. You're not going to find it. And you're not going to find it for cattle work. Cattle should have been worked already. Desperate times call for desperate measures."

"If you and your brothers step foot on my grandpa's ranch, I can't guarantee that he won't just kick you off as soon as he sees you."

"You've warned us. Now, let me call my older brother and see what he says. He may shoot me down too, but I bet we can figure somethin' out. Because if there's one thing Graham hates, it's seeing cattle not get the attention they deserve. Right, Phil?"

"That is true," Phillip reluctantly agreed.

"Hold on a minute." Seth walked away to make a call to Graham.

"He's always been the hopeful one," Phillip whispered.

"And which are you?" Charlie asked.

"Phillip, the black sheep." He shook her hand as she lightly laughed.

"Nice to meet you. I'm Charlotte, the fish out of water."

Phillip grinned as Seth's voice rose. "Graham, it's worth a shot. If he shoos us off, so be it, but I think he'll want to get the work done if he has a willing crew." He shot them a thumbs up. "Right, well, I'll talk to Phillip and Charlie about that. Yeah, she's here right now. Yeah, hold on." He walked towards Charlie and held out the phone and pressed the speaker button. "You're on speakerphone, Graham, so we can monitor what you say," Seth warned.

"Ms. Chandler," Graham greeted, his deep voice tinged with a hint of regret. "When do you need us out there?"

"Oh, um… well, I guess maybe Thursday, if that works for you? That will give me a day to somehow convince my grandpa that y'all are coming."

Graham sighed over the phone. "I suggest you don't. I'd just tell him you hired a crew to come out. That way he'll get what supplies he needs ready for the cows. We'll bring our own horses. Hayes will see to that. We'll clean out the pastures on Thursday and drive them to the pens. We'll work 'em on Friday."

"Mr. Hastings, I—"

"It's Graham, ma'am. And let's just see how this goes. I know you're not promising cupcakes and lemonade. I'll be prepared for the boot in my—"

Phillip cleared his throat loudly to cut his brother off, and Graham took the warning.

"Let's just say I'm prepared if your granddaddy threatens to kill me. I'll let you know, though, I'm not one to shy away from confrontation. We'll get those cows for ya, Ms. Chandler."

He hung up and Seth rolled his eyes at his manners. "You'll have to excuse him. He sometimes forgets how to end a phone call." Seth pocketed his phone. "Well, how's that?"

Charlie's relieved smile held a touch of wonder as she looked at him in complete bafflement. "I don't know why you're willing to help me out, and it may be the death of all of us, but I'm thankful and will just say thanks for risking your neck."

"You're welcome."

"At least we know if all of you get shot down, there will still be a continuation of the Hastings line." Phillip pointed to himself on a laugh.

"Phillip's too soft for ranch work," Seth teased.

Not one to get his feathers ruffled, Phillip only laughed. "Not my thing, kid. Now go on. Treat Ms. Charlie to a Sloppy's steak while you're both in town, or Ruby will be offended."

Seth pointed towards the door, grabbing his hat off the counter. "That alright with you, Charlie?"

"Well, I should really be getting back."

"Oh, come on now, you owe me," Seth said. "I just hooked you up with an entire workforce. The least you can do is have a meal with me."

"Grandpa—"

"Is at home, isn't he? And doesn't he have an awesome Julia casserole to heat up for supper?"

"I did leave it warming in the oven," she admitted.

"See? Perfect. Come on. Slop's probably already got our meal a cookin'."

"Ruby," Phillip corrected, and Seth snapped his fingers.

"Right. I keep forgetting we're to work on calling her by her real name now. Oops. Don't tell Lawrence." He grinned at his brother as he hurried to the door and opened it for Charlie.

~

Charlie had yet to eat at the local diner. To be honest, she had actually avoided it. It looked dingy and old, and essentially just not that appetizing. But what it lacked in exterior, it more than made up for on the interior. It was clean, perhaps a bit outdated in its furnishings, but incredible smells drifted from the kitchen and that had her following Seth to a small table for two by the window.

A beautiful woman she recognized from the bridal party of Julia's wedding walked up and slapped Seth on top of the head with the laminated menu. "Hey, knucklehead," she greeted warmly. "I don't see you in town solo very often. What brings you in?"

Seth's cheeks flushed. "She means I'm usually with my brothers."

Ruby, aware that she'd made it sound like he ventured to town with other people all the time, not specifically stating his brothers, also corrected herself. "Yes, that's what I meant."

"I was over at Phil's and then Charlie walked in. I thought I'd treat her to dinner."

Charlie's face blanched. "Oh, you don't have to buy me dinner. I didn't realize—"

"My treat. Ruby here is my brother Lawrence's fiancé. Another pretty lady who lost her mind." He shook his head as if Ruby were a lost cause.

She swatted him again on a laugh and he pulled away. "Hey now, don't spread whatever it is you got. The love bug seems to be catchin', and I don't want it."

Ruby rolled her eyes and looked to Charlie. "What can I get you, Charlie?" Realizing she'd forgotten to let the woman look at the menu in her hand, she handed it over. "You want a steak or a burger tonight, Seth?"

"Definitely a chicken fried steak. I'm starving."

"Sides?"

"Whatever is easiest."

"I like that kind of order." Ruby turned towards Charlie. "You decide?"

"I'll just have the same." She handed the menu back to Ruby and watched as she hurried back into the kitchen.

"Ruby's great. We grew up together here in Parks. She and Law have been friends since they were in diapers and then all of a sudden, last year they realized they were fools over one another." He grinned. "Pretty crazy. Same thing happened to my brother Cal and Alice Wilkenson. I'm telling you, my brothers are droppin' like flies."

She smiled at that and accepted the glass of sweet tea Ruby placed on the table. She took a long sip. "I think that's sweet."

"Yeah, Slop can get it a little too sweet sometimes."

"No, not the tea. I meant about your brothers."

"Oh, right." Seth smirked. "I guess so. It's definitely changed the dynamics on the ranch now. Graham actually calls it quits at a decent hour so he can go home to Julia. Calvin finds more excuses to visit Sheffield during the week to pop in on Alice. Phillip travels to Midland every other weekend to see Helena. Lawrence and Ruby hang out *all the time*, and I should know, because Lawrence and I are roommates. And then my brother Hayes fell for this real pretty hairdresser in Sheffield named Alejandra. She's got a cute little daughter named Ava who seems to have us all wrapped around her pinky. And then just recently, Clint, of all people, fell for a game warden. Bailey almost arrested him once." Seth chuckled at that memory before taking a sip of his own drink.

"And what about you?" Charlie asked. "Anyone special for you?"

"Nope. Not yet anyway. I've avoided the bug. Probably because I rarely leave the ranch. It's safe out there. What about you? You moved to Parks and left where?"

"Dallas area."

"Dallas?" His brows lifted. "A city girl moving to the Chandler's Crossing Ranch. Wow."

"I grew up visiting the ranch, but yes, it's a big change."

"Why'd you do it?"

She dipped her straw in and out of her drink and shrugged. "Someone needed to see about Grandpa."

"And that somebody had to be you?"

"Well, no." She met his gaze to see what he would think of her response. "But I think I'm the only one willing."

Empathy stared back at her, and she liked that he didn't start insulting her grandpa. Instead, he said, "That's a little sad to hear."

"Tell me about it."

"Do you miss Dallas?"

"Every day." She replied honestly. "Every. Single. Day. Though I'm trying not to. I'm just running out of patience, I think. But I have to stick it out. I have to take over the ranch so that it stays in the family."

"That's a lot of pressure to put on yourself."

"Well, I don't have six brothers stepping up or helping out. My cousins don't want it. My parents definitely don't."

"And you do?"

"I think so. I don't want to see it sold. I love the ranch. Though I'm a bit overwhelmed when I think about how much I need to learn. But I'll get there. It will just take time."

"Have you considered hiring a manager or a foreman?"

She nodded. "I have, actually. But when I pitched the idea to Grandpa, he threw a fit and refused to speak to me about the ranch for two days, which obviously makes it hard to learn when your only teacher isn't speaking to you." She leaned back in her seat as Ruby placed a large platter in front of her. "Whoa."

Grinning, Seth looked up at Ruby adoringly. "I think you won her over, Slop."

Ruby grinned before heading to check on other customers.

"This is huge." Charlie reached for her napkin and Seth lightly grabbed her hand. She paused, curious and a bit unnerved by his touch.

"Mind if I say grace right quick?" Seth asked.

"Not at all." She relaxed her hand, but he didn't release it. Instead, he bowed his head, said a quick prayer, and then gently squeezed her hand on the "Amen" before letting go.

"Don't tell Julia, but nothing beats Ruby's chicken fried steak." Seth cut a bite off and waited until Charlie did the same and they both slipped their first bites in their mouths at the same time. He watched as her eyes sparkled a moment. "Yep, you just tasted the best thing in your life. Glad I got to see it."

A soft giggle escaped her lips as she eagerly cut a second piece off the creamy and crunchy battered steak. "This is amazing."

"Now that you're in the area you'll be able to come eat one any time you want."

"If I did that, I'd gain a hundred pounds."

"Nah." He smirked. "You'll work it off." He patted his own flat stomach.

"I want to thank you for reaching out to your brother about the cattle work. I know my grandpa isn't going to like it. And I may be homeless after he rages about it and kicks me off the ranch, but we need the help right now. The ranch... well, it just doesn't look or run like it used to. It's kind of sad to see."

"Sometimes old cowboys can get so caught up in their prejudices that they miss something great right in front of them. And that can lead to things, or them, fallin' apart. My brother, Graham, is a prime example. He loves the 7H. It's his whole life, and then when Julia arrived, he chomped on her all the time. He hated being around her. He hated that she was there and in the way. But then something about her just kept pickin' at him until he fell totally in love. Now it's as if she was the one thing missing from his life and none of us can imagine Graham without her. Maybe your grandpa will see how valuable you can be, and he'll come around."

"I hope you're right. But I don't know how to show him my value right now since I don't know much. That's why I was working in the garden the other day. My grandmother used to have the most beautiful and lush garden. So many of my memories of the ranch were in that garden with her or shelling peas on the front porch or shucking corn. I thought if I could just do *something* productive and meaningful, something I at least know a little about and clean up around the place, he'd be excited about the possibilities." She twirled her fork in the green beans on her plate. "I just don't know."

"Well, you know what, you have friends now. Anything you need, just reach out to us," Seth encouraged. "I don't care if your name is Chandler. I'm so far removed from that rivalry and family hatred, I just don't factor it into my opinion. Land is land and needs to be taken care of. People are people and they need tending too. So, if you need help with your garden, just ask. Annie taught me everything she knows, and that's a lot."

Relieved and impressed with his unbiased approach towards her, she raised her tea. "Then here's to a new Chandler-Hastings relationship. May we be friends, neighbors, and garden experts together."

He laughed and clinked his glass with hers. "You know what?" he reached down beside his chair for the sacks of seeds he grabbed from Phillip. "I've got seeds for some of my fall planting right here. I could spare some if you want some to try out."

"You saw my plot, it's nowhere near ready for planting."

"Sure it is. You've got a corner, don't you?"

"A very *small* corner spot cleared."

"That's enough then for you and your grandpa. Won't be much to store or can, but it will at least get you started."

"I don't even know if the dirt is ready for new growth. It's been so bogged down with weeds and brush." Charlie waved away his offer.

"I think you underestimate how easy it is to grow things. Just water them. Add a little fertilizer. Here, hold on a second." He stood and walked over to Ruby at the bar, and she disappeared into the kitchen and returned with a handful of small plastic storage bags. He walked over and began sorting some of his seeds into the bags and labeling them with a black marker. "There."

He handed her the various bags and she bit back the emotion she felt rising in her chest at the unbridled kindness Seth continued to show her. Hastings men were terrible people, or so she'd been taught. They were nothing but trouble, liars, and cheats. But she knew deep down that was a lie. In all her recent encounters, not one of the brothers had been rude to her. And here they were offering to help her and her grandpa, knowing full well their presence would not be welcome or appreciated. And then the seeds. Her bottom lip quivered a minute as she took the seeds with shaky hands. "Thanks."

"No problem." He smiled and motioned towards her plate. "You done?"

She nodded and stood as he did. She reached for her purse, and he shook his head. "It's taken care of."

"You just gave me seeds and you booked me a crew for cattle work. I think I can pay for my own meal, Seth."

"Nope. It's on whichever brother has the largest tab with Ruby. It's sort of our agreement." He grinned mischievously and she laughed.

"How very little brother of you."

"Well, they owe me for all the years of picking on me. Come on, probably time you make it home or your grandpa's going to think you got lost."

"And we'd hate for him to come and find me here." She cringed and feigned a grimace.

"That is for sure true. I like my hide intact, thanks."

Smiling, she followed him outside and back towards their vehicles across the street. She unlocked the doors to her SUV, and he politely opened her door. "It's been fun talking with you, Charlie. I'll see you in a couple days."

"You too. Thanks again." He slipped his cowboy hat onto his head and walked towards his truck, his long legs eating up the distance in just a few short steps. She noticed he was slightly bow-legged and found that kind of cute as it added a bit of a swagger to his walk. She'd also noticed, when he'd held her hand to say grace, that her pulse had jumped at the contact. And that when he looked at her with those sharp blue eyes, she had a hard time remembering what she was thinking or saying. Nervous about that, Charlie quickly turned the key and reminded herself that even though Seth Hastings was kind and nice to look at, he was still a Hastings. And though she didn't have the same prejudice towards him as her grandpa, she still had to tread carefully so as not to upset her family.

H

Chapter Five

Seth patted the side of Trisket's neck as he waited for Hayes to finish hanging his tack in the tack room, his brother prepping for their work over at Chandler's Crossing for the following day. When Hayes walked out, however, Seth noticed him nervously moving from one task to the next in jumbled steps and clumsy hands. "Something wrong, Hayes?"

Hayes looked up and shook his head. "Nope. Not at all. Why?" He placed his hands on his hips and his eyes darted around the barn as if looking for something else to work on. "How's Trisket? Antsy? Does she need time in the pens?" He walked over to Graham's horse and rubbed a hand down her snout.

"Trisket is fine." Seth narrowed his eyes. "But you're not. What gives?"

"I said I'm okay. Just... nervous."

"About what?"

"Nothing."

"It's more than nothin' if you're wandering around the stables looking for chores. Shall I go fetch a toothbrush so you can scrub the grain in the wood of all the stalls?"

Hayes paused in his pacing and placed a hand over his chest. "You're right, I am losing it." He took his hat off his head and swiped the sweat off his forehead before setting it back. "I'm just... my heart feels like it's going ninety miles per hour, and I can't catch my breath. I'm sweatin' and lightheaded." Hayes walked toward a wooden bench and sat.

Concerned, Seth walked toward him. "Do I need to take you into town? Call Alice? The hospital?"

"No, no, I'll be fine. It's been like this all day."

"Well, that's not normal." Seth sat beside him and studied him warily. "You're not having a heart attack, are you? Or stroke? Or whatever?"

"I-I don't think so." Hayes looked at him. "I mean, no. No, I'm not. Again, I'm just nervous."

"About what?" Seth asked.

"I can't say." Hayes hopped to his feet and walked towards the stall next to Trisket, reached in and rubbed a hand over his own horse, Flash.

"Why not? If it's a health issue, we all need to know about it."

"It's not," Hayes assured him.

"A crazy heart pace, sweating, and about to pass out. I think it's a health issue, Hayes. I mean, you remember at church when Mr. Keith collapsed in the aisle during altar call? That was a heart problem he didn't even know he had."

"Mr. Keith was eighty-five years old," Hayes reminded him.

"Yeah, but still."

"It's not my heart. Well, it is, but not like that."

"I am officially so confused," Seth said slowly.

"I'm going to ask Alejandra to marry me. Tonight," Hayes blurted out.

Seth leaned back, eyes wide at the abrupt announcement. "I see."

"Yeah, so there's that." Hayes waved a hand from his mouth to the air, as if guiding his announcement out into the open.

"I could see how that'd be a bit nerve-wracking."

"Well, yeah. She could say no."

"But she won't."

"But she could," Hayes continued as if not hearing him, and Seth watched as his brother picked up his pacing once again, Flash's ears twitching at the nervous energy coming from his owner. "I mean, we haven't been together that long. She has Ava to consider. She'd have to move out here to the ranch. There's a lot she'd have to figure out."

"But she loves you," Seth added. "And you love her and Ava, and I think that's what's most important to remember."

"Of course I love her. I'd be an idiot not to. I mean, she just— wow, I don't even know where to begin. Yes, I love her." He slowed down his chattering. "I wasn't planning on dating anyone and here she comes. I wasn't planning on marrying anyone any time soon, and then here she comes with her dark eyes, glossy hair, and sassy Spanish. And then Ava—" He fisted a hand to his heart. "That little girl has just won my heart. I love them both, but I don't want to scare her away. She's been through a lot, you know? Well, you don't. But she has. And I don't want Ali to think I'm rushing or pushing her into something, because I'm not. I could be engaged to her forever and still count myself the luckiest man on earth. Though really, a lifelong engagement wouldn't be ideal," he muttered, his words trailing off as he continued his back and forth with himself.

Seth sat grinning as he saw movement from the corner of his eye. Ali stood in the doorway, her eyes watching Hayes curiously, oblivious to the conversation that had been happening before her arrival. Hayes had no idea of her presence, and Seth couldn't wait to see what unfolded. So he did what younger brothers did best: he poked the bear. "So, you're worried Ali will say no if you ask her, but then you're also worried that she'll say yes, because then you're worried she will think it's too fast and want to take things slow, but you're okay with that, but not really?"

"Exactly." Hayes rested both hands on the gate to Flash's stall and leaned his head down to take a deep breath. "I just don't want to screw this up. I've got the ring. Shoot, I've had it for months now. I've invited her over for supper to ask her tonight."

"Got a romantic dinner planned?" Seth asked.

"Of course." Hayes continued hanging his head, breathing in deeply and audibly exhaling.

Seth chuckled. "You're going to die before you can ask her if you don't calm down." Ali walked into the barn and quietly sat next to Seth, her eyes glassy. Seth patted her hand and winked. "Look, you can practice on me if that will help calm your nerves."

"I'm not practicing on you. I've rehearsed it a thousand times in my head today and to Flash," Hayes' hand absentmindedly rose from the stall door to pat his horse's nose.

"Well, then, let's hear it."

"No. I only want to tell her. I want it to be special. Something just between us."

"And Flash," Seth reminded him.

"Seth—" Annoyed, Hayes turned to face his little brother and paused when he saw Alejandra sitting beside him. Her watery smile had him frozen in place.

"Mi vaquero," she whispered.

Seth rose to his feet. "I think I'll just leave you two alone." He lightly kissed Ali's cheek. "Take pity on him, Ali. He's about to die."

With a happy sob, Ali darted towards Hayes and jumped into his arms.

~

The morning held a slight briskness, the small whisper of promised cooler weather that only Octobers can give. Oh, the weather would tease them for a few days, giving them fall-like temperatures in the mornings and evenings, and then it would turn blazing hot again until November. But cold snaps were refreshing, and Charlie couldn't wait for more. She sat nervously on the front porch in one of the wooden rocking chairs that needed a fresh sanding and paint job and added that to her long running list of to-dos. Her grandpa, still unaware that the crew she hired would be the entire Hastings brothers fleet, sat beside her glancing at his watch every few minutes.

"What time did you tell them?"

"They'll be here, Grandpa." Relief loosened the knots of her stomach when she saw a truck and trailer coming up the drive. "There they are." When it pulled to a stop, Hayes Hastings stepped out, tipping his hat towards her. Her grandpa didn't seem to know who the man was, which was good, but when Graham Hastings stepped out of the passenger side, Bob Chandler was on his feet and appeared at her side quicker than the Holy Spirit.

"What are you doing here?" he barked, looking repulsed at the handshake between Graham and Charlie.

Charlie turned to face her grandpa as more and more Hastings brothers continued to arrive. "Well, we needed help and I couldn't find a crew. The

Hastings family offered to come and help us out. Seemed like the logical choice."

"What information can you give us about the cattle, Mr. Chandler?"

"I'm not tellin' you anything about my cows, you thief. Probably here to see what all I have so you can take them for yourself."

Surprisingly calm, Graham only stood and took the insult in stride. "I assure you we are stretched as far as we can go with cattle and the grass to graze them, so they're safe from us."

"Says you," Chandler combatted. "You're a Hastings. Can't trust a word you say, boy."

Graham turned his attention to an embarrassed Charlie. "Ms. Chandler, you have some direction for us?"

"Thankful that her grandpa had divulged his entire plan the previous evening due to him expecting a workforce this morning, Charlie gave Graham the rundown. "The pens are out this way." She motioned for him to walk with her, and they left a staring Bob Chandler in the middle of the yard.

"Sorry about that," Charlie whispered.

Graham's lips tilted. "It wasn't as bad as I thought it would be, so we'll count ourselves lucky."

"I guess you're right." Her eyes darted to Seth's truck parking next to Lawrence's and watched him meet up with his brothers and immediately start helping unload the horses.

Graham smirked. "I like to keep a few on horseback and a few at the pens. Seth's good at working the pens, so I'll probably leave him here with Lawrence. The rest of us will start on the back side of the property over there and push the rest of them this way. When we feel we have a good lead on them, we'll work them towards the pens. Any loose stragglers, I'll send Hayes and Cal after them. But I think we need to focus on the bulk of the herd first, get some numbers from Bob afterwards and go from there."

"I am honestly okay with whatever you think is best. I don't know much about this. Where would you like me? At the pens?" Her eyes landed upon Seth again and she hoped she was near him just for the cheerful support he seemed to always offer.

"That's a great idea. He and Lawrence will be able to walk you through what's happening in the various stages, how to rotate the cows once they're in the pens, and why we do that. You'll be an expert by the end of the day, Ms. Chandler."

"Charlie, please. And thank you. I'd like to be as close to one as I can get."

"One thing to add to that." Graham darted a gaze towards Bob Chandler as he kept waving for his brothers to stop unloading horses and shouting orders for them to turn themselves around and leave. "If you could keep him somewhat calm, that'd be helpful."

"That might be harder than herding cows."

Graham chuckled. "You're probably right about that. It's one reason I'm taking Clint with me. He can only handle someone barkin' at him for so long before he barks back. I don't want to escalate the situation any further than we already have."

"I appreciate that."

"Julia and some of the girls are going to bring lunch about noon."

Her brows lifted. "Oh, I didn't even consider that."

"She wanted to. She also wanted to see you and force your grandpa into more conversation." He smiled at his wife's tenacity. "Best not argue with her once she sets her mind on something."

"Wise man." Charlie smiled as Hayes walked up.

"We're ready when you are, Graham."

"Alright." He extended his hand to Charlie again and she hesitantly shook it as she watched him plop a dusty cowboy hat on his head and huddle with his brothers.

Seth walked her direction as most of his brothers saddled up. "I hear you're on pen duty?"

"If you'll have me."

"Of course. Show us the way, Ms. Charlie."

Lawrence walked with them and warily eyed Bob as they passed by him. "You coming, Mr. Chandler?" he offered in a friendly tone.

"You bet I'm coming, you weas—"

"Grandpa," Charlie warned, shooting a disappointed and spark-filled gaze at Bob that had him taking a surprised and cautious step back at being interrupted and silenced by his once acquiescent granddaughter. But she heard his boots crunching behind them as they walked towards the pens.

Lawrence tested one of the gates, and then walked back to his truck and removed a shovel and hedge trimmers. "We need them to swing a bit easier." He started trimming the overgrown grass, vines, and brush that interfered with the gate's movement. When he was satisfied with that one, he pointed to Seth help him start on the next one. She was impressed that he would put in the extra work of cleaning up the pen area, but Lawrence and Seth didn't seem to mind the extra job.

"We need to make sure we have this one closed before they drive them in here." Lawrence pointed to one of the working pen's gates that would normally lead the already worked cattle into a new pasture. Keeping them contained in the front pasture would allow them to drive them into the working pens tomorrow and do what they needed to before releasing them into the neighboring pasture for what would for the fall and winter.

"They're tearin' up my fence lines." Bob mumbled.

"No, they're not, and you know it. They're cleaning them up so they can be utilized properly." Charlie crossed her arms and looked at her grandpa. "Is it really so bad having the help of your neighbors, Grandpa?"

"It is when their name is Hastings."

"Why? Every Hastings I have met so far has been kind to me, despite me being a Chandler. I'm beginning to think this hatred is one-sided."

"That's what they want you to think, Charlotte. I'm sure they're already plotting ideas on how to manipulate you, win you over, and then buy us out. They're greedy, conniving, and just like their granddaddy and daddy before them. Don't be fooled."

"I'm not fooled, Grandpa. Trust me, I'm seeing things clearly." She held back her huff of aggravation and walked towards the pens.

H

Chapter Six

"*Here they come.*" Seth pointed to the driveway as Julia's car pulled up and parked next to Graham's truck. "Right on time. My stomach was starting to growl." He watched Charlie rush towards the women that climbed out of the little red car and immediately start grabbing food dishes from the trunk. Bob Chandler stepped out of the house, his face etched in its familiar scowl. Julia's face blossomed into a smile. "Afternoon, Mr. Chandler."

"Mrs. Hastings."

"We've brought the sustenance for the day." She beamed as Charlie walked up. "Where would you like us to set up?"

"I have some tables and chairs set up on this side of the house in the shade." She took the stacked dishes in Julia's hands so the soon-to-be-mom could take a break.

"I brought some reinforcements." Julia motioned to the other women over her shoulder and pointed to each of them as she introduced them. "Alice and Ali. And this is Ava, Ali's daughter. Bailey might swing by. I think you know her already, the game warden?"

"Yes, we've met. Thank you all for coming. I haven't heard from the guys yet, so I'm not sure when they will be riding up."

Ali set a large foil pan on the built-in wooden buffet counter. She then set a small cooler next to it. "We made tacos with all the fixings. Thought that would be easiest for them to roll up and take with them or scarf down in a hurry." Her little girl walked up carrying a plastic container with a lid and handed it to her mother. "I made Hay some cookies," she announced. "He's going to be my daddy soon." Ali flushed as the new dazzling ring on her finger glinted. Ali grabbed her mother's hand and held it up for Charlie's inspection. "Asked her to marry him yesterday in the barn."

"Sounds romantic." Charlie looked up at Ali. "Congratulations."

"Gracias."

"Yep, we have another fabulous duo coming into the family." Julia hugged Ava to her side. "Is that Lawrence?" Julia held a hand over her eyes and looked towards the pens. "Lawrence!" she yelled, waving him over.

He jogged their direction. "What can I do for ya, Jewels?"

"I have jugs of tea in the back of the car. Can you grab those?"

"Yes ma'am." He obediently did as she asked.

"All Julia has to do is snap her fingers and all these men turn to mush and wait on her." Alice glanced behind Charlie as Bob rounded the corner to see what was taking place. "Mr. Chandler." Alice extended her hand. His face still held trepidation, but the local veterinarian he'd encountered over the years seemed to tamper down some of his bristling temper.

"Doc. How's your daddy?"

"Oh, he's doin' alright. Stubborn and still popping into the clinic more than he should, but he's doing good. You have a honey-do for me while I'm here? I haven't been out here in a while."

"No, don't reckon I do. Haven't had much need of a vet. Thankfully."

"I won't take offense." Alice smiled.

Little Ava walked up to Bob and in her typical no-nonsense manner sized him up and down with an in-depth perusal. "This your ranch, mister?"

Taken aback by the little girl's willingness to speak to him, he nodded. "It is."

"You lived here a long time?"

"My whole life," he stated.

"Whoa." Ava turned to the other women with pure fascination on her face. "That's a long time, because you're old. Is this your house? Did you build it? Did your daddy build it for you?"

Her rapid-fire questions had Ali stepping forward in apology. "I'm sorry, she is fascinated with all things ranch, cowboy, or farming oriented right now. Ava, why don't you help Julia set out the plates."

"Why? They're paper. They aren't heavy. Do you have a horse, mister?"

"I do."

"Can I see it?"

"Ava, not right now," Ali warned.

"It's just a horse, Momma. I'm great with horses. Hay says I'm a natural." She beamed up at him. "I like the hair on your face. It's white and makes me think of Santa. Are you his brother?"

Charlie tried not to laugh, but Alice didn't hold back her snort at the childlike observation.

"He's not my brother." Bob looked towards the pens as if he were plotting an escape route.

Undeterred, Ava continued. "Santa comes in just a couple months. That's what Mr. Graham told me. And he would know. He knows everything."

Alice rolled her eyes at that comment and Julia laughed.

"And he says I will probably get lots of surprises because I'm always so nice. Do you believe in Santa?" Ava asked.

Bob shifted on his boots and cast a searching look to his granddaughter. No help came from any of the women. "I hear he's a good guy."

Ava's smile bloomed even further, as if confirmation of Santa's reputation from a man as old as Bob meant Santa must be real. She turned hopeful eyes on her mother. "I knew it," she whispered, and Bob's lips twitched before he bit back what could have possibly been a smile. "I'm hoping Momma marries Hay soon so Santa can find me at his house. It's bigger and has more room for toys."

"She has no concept on wedding planning yet," Julia muttered to Ali and they both grinned.

"Did you get married?"

"I did."

"Is your princess here?"

"Not anymore."

"Why not?"

"Ava—" Ali stepped forward and Ava shrugged.

"She died," Bob said shortly.

"I'm sorry." Ava reached for his hand and held it. "I bet she was real nice. Was she pretty?"

"Yes," he said simply, Charlie blown away that the little girl had invisibly locked her grandpa in place for twenty questions.

"I bet she liked your hat and boots. Momma likes Hay's hat and boots. I like them too." She squealed as Lawrence snuck up behind her and scooped her off her feet and threw her over his shoulder. He held her upside down and began walking towards the pens.

"Be right back," he called over his shoulder. "I gotta feed this tasty treat to the cows."

She squealed in protest and giggled, her little feet kicking in the air.

Instead of tossing her into a feed trough, Lawrence set her upright in front of Seth and the youngest Hastings brother knelt before her and handed her a small bundle of grassy weeds.

"Always a lesson to learn." Ali watched in pleasure as her daughter held up one slice of grass and Seth nodded that she'd remembered its name. "They've been trying to teach the both of us various things lately."

"That's good." Charlie motioned to herself. "I might need some of those lessons too."

"You'll catch one," Julia encouraged. "Mr. Chandler, would you like some lunch?"

Bob's eyes blinked as he realized he was staring at the little girl hanging out with her future uncles for too long and shook his head. "No," he stated, his voice gruff. And quietly, as he turned to walk away a hushed "thank you" escaped his lips.

Charlie's wide eyes at the good manners he displayed did not go unnoticed by Alice. "Julia's got a way to whip the tough ones into shape. And Ava is the Robin to her Batman. By the end of the day, your granddaddy is going to be a big pile of mush."

"That'd be quite an achievement."

"It'll happen. You'll see." Alice glanced at her watch. "Where are the guys? I'm starving."

"Graham said noon." Julia looked concerned at the extra half hour that had passed. "I'd call him, but he won't hear it."

"I say we eat without them." Alice walked to fetch a plate. "We can feed Thing 1 and Thing 2 at least." She motioned towards Seth and Lawrence. She held her fingers to her lips and let out a shrill and extremely loud whistle. The brothers' heads popped up and they immediately headed her way when she pointed at the food display. They didn't have to be told twice.

Seth walked over to Charlie. "Well, how's it going? Your grandpa disowned you yet?"

"No, thankfully. In fact, he's been... a little different."

"Good different?"

"I *think* so?" she held up her hands as if unsure and he offered a warm and tender smile that had a small leap in her chest urging her to take a step closer to him.

"Seth," Alice snapped. "Better eat while you can."

His eyes lingered a moment longer on Charlie's face and his cheeks flushed before he accepted the plate Ali extended his way. Ava walked up to her and grabbed her hand. "You can sit with me and Lawrence. He says we're the cool table."

Grinning as Alice swatted the back of his head, Lawrence waved a hand towards the empty chairs across from him and high-fived Ava as she sat to eat her lunch.

Charlie fixed her own plate, and though the offer to sit with Lawrence and Ava was tempting, her feet led her to a different table and to Seth.

~

He was back at the pens in time to see the tip of Graham's hat emerge over the horizon and head their direction. Cows and his brothers rushed towards them. He could hear the yells and whistles and considering they were three hours overdue in bringing the cattle in, and the women had long given up and left, Seth was surprised to see Charlie stepping up beside him. Bob walked up as well and watched as the brother's expertly guided the cows into the designated pens, Seth and Lawrence working quickly on gating them inside. Graham, covered in dust and a soaking wet shirt from sweating, climbed off his saddle, taking a minute to find his legs before walking towards Charlie. His jaw was clenched, his eyes hard, and if Seth didn't know Graham, he'd find his older brother quite intimidating in that moment. Annoyance radiated from his stiff shoulders in waves. To Seth's surprise, his tone was even when he spoke. "We did the best we could. Looks like you may have a few stragglers. We aren't doing those today. We'll do another run through in the morning. The brush is too thick back in the ravines and back pastures. We'll have to send Hayes back in there. And he refuses to use Flash for that task. Plus, he doesn't have split reins for today."

"Alright. How many are we talking about?" Charlie asked.

Graham shrugged. "Don't really know. Couldn't get close enough today, really, without threat to my legs and the horses. I wasn't prepared to ride through brush. None of us were to that extent. Something you might want to consider is some brush control."

"She don't need recommendations from a Hastings," Bob snapped. "We have a brush management plan in place. It takes time."

"I understand that, but these cows are in tough shape. There's not enough grass to feed 'em. What grass you had is gone, either due to the brush invading your pasture lands or due to overgrazing. You need to dwindle your herd until you have more grass," Graham suggested.

"Sell the cows?"

"Not all of them," he stated, ignoring the muttering tantrum Bob Chandler tossed out to all the weary brothers as they climbed down from their horses. "Look," Graham shook his head as if struggling how to word his assessment. "This place needs some serious work. Those cows, even if you sell some right now, are not going to fetch you a decent price because they're in such tough shape. They're underweight. You're going to have to supplement through the winter to get them to a decent enough weight to sell some of them, so you might could break even. I'm not harping on your lands because of your grandpa or what not, I just call it like I see it. If somethin's not done with the place, Charlie, you're going to have a financial and literal mess on your hands."

Worry had her twining her fingers together. "I understand."

Seth walked up and patted Graham on the shoulder. "But we can help you. Right, Graham?"

His oldest brother raised a brow at the suggestion of even more free manpower for such a cause.

"I mean, with the logistics of it all. Maybe we could coordinate some of the work with when we do it. That way, Charlie can learn while doing sort of thing."

"We'll see. Right now, I need a big glass of water and maybe some food." Graham tipped his hat to Charlie and walked off.

"You okay?" Seth asked.

"How? How could Grandpa let it get this bad? If you ask him, the ranch is running fine. The cows are fine. The pastures are fine. Your brother made it sound like everything is definitely not *fine*." She ran a hand through her hair and exhaled a shaky breath. "I don't know what to do. This is all over my head. I don't know how to sell cows. I've never done it. I don't know how to treat brush. I don't know what grasses to plant or hope for. Seth, I'm not going to be able to do this."

Seth gripped her shoulders. "Charlie," He lightly shook her until she looked up at him. "Breathe." He mimicked inhaling and exhaling. "Rome wasn't built in a day. Ranches aren't either. A herd isn't. Things take time. You have to take reasonable bites at a time. You know you have a brush problem. Then look at which pastures offer the most grazing opportunities as they are right now, which means they have less brush," he added for her understanding. "And you work from there. You want more grazing land. Start with what you have and make it better, then move to the next pasture and the next. Modify your herd to utilize what you have. As your grazing lands grow, so does your herd. It might be a loss for now, but in the long run, you'll build it back up. And all will be healthy."

"But—" She shook her head, her eyes turning glassy as tears threatened to fall. "It's too much." Her lips quivered. "I thought I was coming to a ranch that my grandpa had maintained and tended so that he could just teach me how to sustain it. I didn't know I'd have to start from scratch and claw my way out of years of neglect. I'm not equipped to do that."

"Yet," Seth added.

"Seth, please stop being so positive about this. This is bad."

He smirked. "I can't help it. It's my nature to always look at the bright side of things. And one of the bright things Chandler's Crossing has going for it right now, is you. A fresh set of eyes, determination, and willingness. That's what it needs. So I'd say you're the perfect person for the job."

She lifted a hand and gripped one of his that rested on her shoulder. "I can't do this alone, though, and I can't find help."

"You will."

"But Grandpa—"

"Will just have to get over his pride a bit and let you take care of this place," Seth finished. "We'll help as much as we can. That's what neighbors do. What friends do. You're not out here alone, trust me." He tugged her towards him into a friendly hug that settled her head against the middle of his chest, his chin resting on top of her silky blonde hair. He felt her slowly relax, her arms hugging him tighter. Feeling hopeful that he'd helped her gain perspective, his confidence tanked when he caught the watchful and disdain-filled eyes of Bob Chandler over her shoulder.

H

Chapter Seven

Groaning, Clint sat in in the chair next to his girlfriend, Bailey, and gave her a tender kiss of welcome. "Hey, stranger."

"Hey, yourself." She grinned as he groaned again and shifted in his seat. "You going to make it?"

"Just sore from workin' over at Chandler's place today."

"We all are," Calvin added, holding his hand up in a friendly wave as Phillip walked into Sloppy's Diner and towards their long row of tables to join the crew.

"That place is in terrible condition." Hayes shook his head in sympathy. "I had no idea brush that thick even existed around here anymore, much less over there."

"I noticed it a bit last year when I was stalkin' that elk herd in the ravine," Clint added. "But I didn't think Chandler had cattle that far out. Makes absolutely no sense why he would."

"I don't think he knew where all his cows had gone." Graham lifted the cold beer to his lips and savored a long sip. "His tags and numbers were all off according to what Charlie showed me. We have our work cut out for us tomorrow."

"I'm just proud of you guys for helping them." Julia patted Graham's thigh. "I know it's hard to do such work for someone who may not show their gratitude, but you have all stepped up."

"Okay, rainbows and butterflies," Alice waved a hand for Julia to tone down the praise. "The question is, now what? I'd be out there to help you guys record tomorrow, but I've got two canine surgeries in the morning."

"I'm going to let Charlie man the clipboard," Graham stated. "She needs to learn how to do it. It will also directly give her the numbers of how many head they have. Hayes, Lawrence, and Cal will be chasing down the remaining cows in the pastures. Seth, Clint, me, and Charlie will work cows. And if Bob wants to help, he can."

"Is that enough people?" Julia asked concerned.

"It will have to be."

"Anything you need from me?" Phillip asked. "I could probably come out and help in the pens."

"Careful what you volunteer for." Seth stole a French fry from Alice's plate and popped it into his mouth.

"If you're willing, I'll take you," Graham confirmed.

"Is Helena coming up tomorrow?" Julia asked.

"Supposed to be. I'll text her and let her know where I'll be so she isn't hunting me down."

"You're usually only one of two places, Phil. Can't be that hard to find you." Lawrence smirked, briefly standing as Ruby walked over. "You done?"

"For now." She accepted his firm kiss that turned tender when she lightly cupped his face. "There." She patted his cheek. "I think that's given me a new energy boost. It's been busy tonight and my feet are killin' me."

"Take a seat." Lawrence pulled out the chair next to him and Ruby sat.

"I only have ten minutes. Then I need to help Kara again. Hold the phone—" She hopped to her feet and started walking towards the door as Charlotte Chandler walked inside. "Hey, Charlie. Welcome."

Ruby motioned for her to follow her. "Why don't you come sit with us?" She rounded the corner and Charlie took in the full Hastings family seated and waiting for their supper.

"Charlie!" Lawrence welcomed as if they were old friends. He shoved Seth's shoulder. "Scoot over. Come on over here, Chandler, and have a seat."

With no other option, Charlie did as she was asked.

"What can I get you to drink? Water? Tea? A beer?" Ruby asked.

"Or a wine," Julia pointed out.

"Or wine," Ruby added with a smile. "She wants to live vicariously through you."

"I should probably go with water, but I really could use a glass of wine. Red, please."

"On it. I'll bring you both." Ruby hurried off.

"Thanks for letting me join you. I didn't realize you guys would be here."

"None of us felt like making Julia cook us another meal today and Ali suggested Slop's," Clint explained.

"And your daughter, is she here?" Charlie asked.

"No." Ali smiled. "She is enjoying time being spoiled by Annie and Henry while we're in town."

"I see. She was rather cute today and seems to have a way with grumpy old men."

"That she does." Alice pointed her fork at Graham, and he briefly narrowed a glare at her, which only made Alice grin even more.

"You've got nerve, Al," Lawrence warned. "You're almost as old as Graham is."

"Hush your mouth, Lawrence. That is not even close to being true," Alice defended.

Calvin tossed a white napkin of truce between them. "How are you feeling after today, Charlie?" he asked.

She nudged Seth's elbow. "I shared with Seth a bit of my feelings earlier today when I went into full meltdown mode. I'm so grateful to all of you. But I am extremely overwhelmed as well. I won't lie about it. Grandpa hasn't spoken to me all day. He wouldn't even answer me about dinner options. That's why I came here. I couldn't stand being in the house for one more minute."

Seth rested an arm over the back of her chair, his hand gently tugging her towards him in a brief side hug.

"If he knew I was eating with you tonight—"

"He won't," Graham assured her. "We won't tell him. And anytime you need a break, you're always welcome to come to the 7H for a visit."

Impressed her husband offered the invitation, and also loving the idea of more female company, Julia reached across the table and squeezed Charlie's hand. "Definitely come visit."

"The only thing he said to me today after you all left was, 'make sure they find all the cows.' As if that's your responsibility." She shook her head in dismay.

"He's a tough man," Seth chimed in. "Tough men take time to come around to new things. Right, Graham?"

Phillip choked on his sip of tea at Seth calling out their older brother.

"Careful," Graham warned.

"No, but seriously," Seth continued. "Before Julia, Graham was well on his way to becoming a Bob Chandler. You can't deny it, Graham."

"I didn't think I was that bad."

All the brothers sent him doubtful looks and Julia giggled at Graham's embarrassment.

"Graham," Alice butted in. "You were awful."

"Thank you for sugar-coating it, Alice."

"You wouldn't be my friend if I did. Now, where is our supper. These fries are only holding me over for so long. And then there's going to be a special dessert, because we need to celebrate Hayes and Ali." She smiled at the newly engaged couple.

~

"I can't believe you two are engaged." Seth shook his head. "Graham, Hayes, Lawrence... the ranch is filling up with females mighty quick."

"Speaking of," Alice pointed her fork at him. "You'd better get after building that house of yours. Because once Lawrence and Ruby are married, I doubt they'll want you as their roomie."

"You're building a house?" Charlie asked.

"Sort of." Seth smiled. "It's been a work in progress the last couple of years. I haven't settled on anything yet. I just have a site cleared and leveled."

"If you keep dragging your feet it won't get done," Clint warned. "Trust me. It took forever for me to jump into the project of my own. But I'm glad I did." He winked at Bailey as if with the promise of a future in his home.

"I know." Seth shrugged his shoulders. "It's just hard to think about what I want for long-term there. What if my future wife doesn't like what I choose?"

"Future wife?" Calvin chuckled.

"Yeah. I plan on getting married one day," Seth pointed out. "What if she hates my house? It's not like we can house shop somewhere else, because we're on the ranch."

"You're putting too much pressure on yourself," Bailey assured him. "Just think about what you need and then add a little extra room for growth."

"And a big kitchen," Julia suggested.

"Definitely." Ali nodded and then grinned at Hayes with eyes full of warmth that everyone knew meant she approved of her future home.

"See, lots to consider. Unless Law wants to build a new house and I just keep his." Seth forced a toothy smile at Lawrence and his older brother shook his head. "Not on your life. I like my house."

"You still have some time." Julia nodded towards Lawrence. "Unless Lawrence and Ruby are getting married quicker than we realize." She narrowed her eyes on the brother and he shook his head.

"And I guess I could always move to Clint's in the meantime."

"Sure, just invite yourself over." Clint rolled his eyes.

"Or Cal's," Alice offered.

Calvin, liking his quiet home and space, looked annoyed at her suggestion. She grinned.

"What I suggest, Charlie, getting back to the previous topic—" Graham still hung up on their conversation about her grandpa and her ranch, waited for the table to quiet. "You need to hire a foreman. You need someone there to manage the operations of that place."

"I know. I was thinking the same thing, but Grandpa won't hear of it right now. He is the foreman in his mind."

"But he's not fulfilling the role. Not even close," Calvin said. "And a man like Bob Chandler seems like the kind that will look at something in a very black and white manner. Yes, it's his place, but he knows he needs help. That's the only reason we're sitting here tonight. If he didn't need us on his property, he would have shot a few warning shots until taking aim to be rid of us for good. He *knows* he needs help. He doesn't want to ask for it. He may not even want to admit it, but he knows. If you approach him from a budgetary standpoint, perhaps he'll listen."

"Budgetary? What do you mean?"

Cal leaned his elbows on the table to angle his body more her direction so as to be heard. "Look at the finances. If there's enough to bring on a foreman, which I'm assuming there is, because you can tell by riding around that place there hasn't been an active crew out there in a while, then suggest bringing on a manager. Salaried. It might pull some purse strings a bit tighter, but I think it will pay off having someone actively running the place. Bob may think he is, but by the state of the cattle and the pastures, he's fooling himself. And I think he inwardly knows that too."

"I do have access to all the books. That is one thing he didn't mind pawning off on me. I'll look it over and see what I can find."

"If you need help, just ask." Graham offered.

"I will. Thank you. Thanks to all of you. I'm honestly shocked I'm sitting at a table with the Hastings family right now. This was so untoward growing up. I remember when I'd come visit my grandparents and see you guys at church up at the front, I always wondered what you were like. Because from my view, you never seemed as mean or horrible as what my grandpa coached me in thinking."

"You'll learn real quick, Charlie, that I'm the best." Lawrence winked at her as Phillip shoved his shoulder.

Relaxing back into her chair, she bumped into Seth's arm that he still had draped there. She straightened a moment before she realized it was him and then settled back again. He smelled the fruity scent of her hair and wondered what girly bottle of shampoo that must have come from. Was it pink? Turquoise? Something overly feminine that clashed with the rustic atmosphere she had dropped herself into? He liked to think it was and that it did. He liked Charlie. He liked that she would move across the state to see about her family and family legacy and want to make it better. He liked that she was open about not knowing what she was doing and that she needed help. She didn't try to fluff herself up. She was real, honest, and, if he were honest with himself, real pretty. He remembered how she felt in his arms yesterday. He felt the slight tug of attraction that warmed his belly when she'd wrapped her arms around him. He wasn't dumb, he knew when he felt the beginnings of something brewing. And though he'd kept himself single for most of his life, he knew when he liked someone. And Charlotte Chandler was well on her way to wiggling her way into his line of sight. He'd already found that he'd reminded himself four times that she was a Chandler and he was a Hastings and that her grandpa would die before letting her date a Hastings. But even reminding himself for the fifth time about her grandpa's disapproval didn't keep his fingers from lightly dancing through the tips of her ponytail as she sat. And as with all upsides that he tried to find in life, his hopeful heart thought that maybe, just maybe, family prejudices wouldn't matter anymore in the future. That perhaps the Hastings and Chandlers could coexist. That maybe, even if it took some work, that mended bridge could start with he and Charlie being friends.

H

Chapter Eight

There were mornings Charlie woke up and missed being in Dallas. She missed the night shift, which she never thought she'd say. She missed the busyness of a crowded emergency room, which was odd to say. She also felt bad that she missed emergencies. Perhaps, she thought, it was because she hadn't felt needed on the ranch. She thought she'd come and jump right into the nitty gritty details and lifestyle of running the ranch. That wasn't the case. She was held at an arm's length from any of the inner workings to the point that she felt completely useless. She *needed* to feel useful. Instead, she struggled motivating her feet to walk the hallway towards the kitchen.

She could already hear her grandpa pouring his first cup of coffee and she dreaded the cold shoulder morning welcome where she would greet him as cheerfully as she could muster and he'd answer, on a good day, with a grunt or his usual silence.

She walked into the kitchen and her grandpa stood with his back to her. "Good morning."

Without turning around and slowly mixing his heavy cream into his coffee cup along with a splash of something extra, Bob Chandler's shoulders tensed. "Your *crew* is here," he remarked drily.

"Oh." She peeked through the curtains out the window over the sink and watched as the Hastings men began unloading their horses. "Good. I know they were wanting to look for the lost cows."

"They aren't lost." Grandpa turned towards her, his eyes serious. "They're just out in the brush. Easy work."

"Either way, they have to be found in order to be worked. Graham said he'd like to finish everything today."

"I bet he does."

Charlie prayed for patience and went about making her own coffee in a travel mug so she'd could hurry outside. "Grandpa, I'm going to be frank with you this morning." She turned towards him and waited until she had his attention. He eyed her, his eyes still void of any sort of sign of what his thoughts might be. "You're being a jerk. There, I said it. Now, I'm sorry if that hurts your feelings. I'm not trying to. I'm just pointing out the obvious. I get it, you don't like the Hastings family. Trust me, I *get* it. You've told me a million times since I was a kid. But right now, I don't care. I don't hate them. I probably never will. It's not in my nature to hate anyone. And guess what, right now especially, in this moment, I'm thankful for them. Not only have they been the only decent conversation I've had in months, but they're here doing work for *free* that we need them to do. They didn't hackle over coming to Chandler's Crossing. They didn't grumble about how much they hate you. In fact, it's been quite the opposite. They don't mention hatred at all, other than it seems to be part of the family history. So I'm asking you, even if it is just for today, to keep your surly attitude, hateful remarks, and ungratefulness to yourself. We need them today. If you cannot contain the above, I'm asking you to stay in the house and take a day off from ranch duties." Charlie huffed a breath and walked to the screen door that that led to the side yard, not even waiting for a response from her grandpa.

Seth spotted her first and offered a friendly wave of good morning, followed by Calvin, who tipped his hat. Neither left their work, but went back to their responsibilities. Graham walked towards her, his presence less intimidating by the day as she got to know him. He gave her a friendly nod at his approach. "Hayes, Calvin, and Seth will be heading out to the back pasture to gather up the last few cows. Lawrence, Clint, Phillip, and I will get started on working what's here. I hate to not do them all at once, but I'm trying to save us some time and knock out the bulk of the work before it starts heating up."

"I understand." Charlie's head bobbed up and down as she agreed, and she twisted her hands together in front of her as she watched the three Hastings brothers on horseback make their way across the ranch. She knew their task would not be easy, but all seemed confident. Graham handed her a clipboard. "What is this?"

"I reckon you need to learn how to work cows, Ms. Charlie," Graham stated, a little quirk to the corner of his mouth telling her he thought the idea of her doing such work might be funny. "We can show you how we do it. That should give you a picture of what needs to be done and you can adjust your approach later on down the road if you want."

"Oh." She smiled in thanks. "Sounds great. I warn you, though, I don't even know what to write down."

"I'll walk you through it." Graham motioned for her to follow him towards the pens, and she fell into step beside him, though she had to take two extra steps to keep up with his long stride. He stopped abruptly before reaching the pens. "Oh, and I'm going to warn you—"

"Yes?" she asked.

"I can be... well, apparently I'm not the nicest person when I work cows. Just a warning. I don't mean anything by it. It's just I like to get things done. The right way."

"Warning noted. You forget, I live with Bob Chandler. I can handle difficult men."

He harumphed and a quick flash of a smile crossed his face before he turned back towards the pens. Appreciating his honesty, Charlie listened as he began barking orders at his brothers.

~

Seth didn't mind riding horses. He'd been on the back of one since he was a toddler, but the unstable ground of Chandler's Crossing was new and nerve-racking. He tried to remain relaxed so that his horse wouldn't pick up on his nervous jitters, but he watched as Hayes, on the back of one of his oldest work horses, Rooney, stumbled over the rough terrain as well. Calvin was behind, slow and steady, as was his usual way.

"I don't like this," Cal's voice carried towards them. "We don't know the terrain, and this brush is beyond ridiculous. Chandler should be ashamed of himself for letting his place go like this."

"Just take it easy," Hayes encouraged. "We don't want the horses to feel scared or nervous."

"They're going to have some serious scratches from all this blackbrush," Seth commented.

"They're trained to withstand it. And we'll treat anything that's serious. They're tougher than you give them credit for." Hayes continued to lead and pulled back on the reins and brought Rooney to a halt. He pointed towards a far corner. "There's a few there."

"Great." Calvin reached for his binoculars. "Looks like five."

"Check those trees." Hayes pointed and Calvin turned his attention towards the west. "Yep, two more."

"A few stragglers, my rear." Seth shook his head in disappointment. "I thought it would be like three or four."

"Not much difference either way." Hayes pointed to the five. "You two head that way. I'll get the ones in the trees."

Seth's horse stumbled and quickly righted itself, Cal's horse's ears twitching in response. "Whoa now," he cooed. "Slow and steady."

"You think Bob will help them work cows?" Seth asked curiously.

"Probably not. I have a feeling he will watch from afar just to look for any flaws in Graham's system."

"Pretty sad, if you think about it." Seth tightened his grip on his split reins as he shifted in the saddle. "He's got to be lonely. Even with Charlie here, she says he barely talks to her."

"He is how he wants to be." Cal didn't seem too bothered by the Chandler family dynamics, but Seth couldn't let it go.

"She's his granddaughter. You'd think he'd be more grateful she was willing to move out here with him when the rest of his family refuses to."

Cal angled his head towards Seth and smirked. "You seem awfully invested in Charlie's well-being."

Shrugging, Seth tried to add a little aloofness to his tone. "Just think it's weird is all."

"Right. Well, if she doesn't like the life here with Bob, she can go back to the city. No one is stopping her."

"But then no one would be able to take over the land for her family."

Cal shrugged. "Their problem. Not ours. Generational shifts in land management are always tricky. Can't blame her if it's not right for her. Can't blame his kids either if he's treated them like he treats everyone else."

"It's sad," Seth reiterated. "I can't imagine life without the 7H. I mean, what if we could partner with Chandler or something? Revitalize the ranch and what not."

"We are helping. Right now." Cal pointed to his horse. "And right now, I'm trying not to be ticked off at Chandler for the state of these pastures and the risks we are taking, so my 'feeling sorry' for the Chandlers radar is a bit skewed at the moment."

They traipsed closer toward the cows in silence a few minutes before Seth spoke up again. He didn't like the quiet, and Cal seemed to live in it. "Charlie's pretty though, isn't she?"

He didn't see his brother's smile as Cal quickly turned at the sound of Hayes' calls. They turned their horses to see Hayes in a trot attempting to cut off one of the cows and herd it closer to its friends, but the thickness of the brush and the trees his direction were limiting him.

"Ours aren't going anywhere." Cal tapped his heels into his horse's flanks to trot towards Hayes. "Let's help him dig them out and lead them this way."

Not able to speed up faster than a lope, Seth and Calvin watched in horror as Hayes lifted his reins to stabilize his horse on a surprise jump over a ravine. Feeling the wrongness of the jump, they watched as Hayes released the reins and shifted to jump, all knowing the only way Rooney could stabilize on the other side was without the weight of Hayes on his back. Rooney makes the jump, though he falls on his side, Hayes' leg catching beneath the weight of the horse before Rooney scrambles to find his footing on the slick rock on the other side. Hayes, to their dismay, scrambles to catch himself, but falls into the ravine. There was no stopping the slip or the fall. Horse whinnying and rocks crumbling, a scream pierced the air as Hayes disappeared out of sight.

Calvin dismounted at a sprint, Seth reaching for his brother's horse to try and keep both horses tame. He slid to the ground and tied both their horses to a tree with clumsy hands. His heart sank as he watched Calvin recoil at the sight at the bottom of the ravine before he began searching for a way down. Seth grabbed his arm to stop him, catching a glimpse of an injured Hayes and blood. Lots of blood. "No. I'll go down. You call Graham."

"I've got this—" Calvin struggled against Seth's hold, boots slipping on the rocks and his face already paling.

"Cal, you can't handle a nick on your chin when it bleeds. You're no good if you pass out down there with him. I'll go down. You get the others and get some help. Ride until you have a cell signal. Get Graham to call a helicopter!" Seth called over his shoulder as he clambered down the slope of the ravine, his hands gripping loose rock and vines to help guide him down. Calvin darted away and Seth focused on his other brother. "Well, when you decide to crash you really make it fancy." Breathless and heart pounding, Seth knelt by Hayes to assess his injuries. Panting, Hayes opened his eyes and started to rise, but immediately collapsed against the rocky bottom. "Don't move, brother. You've got a nasty cut. Now hold on. Cal went to get help."

"I-I can't m-move my legs."

Though that announcement jolted Seth, he prayed he could keep a calm face for Hayes. "Probably just the shock of it all. You're going to be just fine. I don't know what I can do for ya right now other than try to get this bleeding to stop."

"I can barely b-breathe. My lungs." Hayes pressed a hand to his chest and Seth gripped it.

"Just take slow and steady breaths. We aren't going anywhere for a while, so we have all the time in the world to get your lungs back to their normal routine. Try to take as deep a breath as you can." He leaned his head against his brother's chest and silently thanked the Lord they sounded normal. No punctures that he could tell. He didn't have a single thing on him to stop the bleeding of Hayes' leg, and he certainly didn't know how he was to accomplish that task when he saw bone. Mustering his courage, Seth released his hold on Hayes's hand. "I'm going up to my horse. I've got my extra shirt in my saddle bag. We can use that to stop the bleeding. Hang on, alright? I'll be right back." Hayes' grip on his hand didn't loosen and Seth felt horrible prying himself free, but his brother's face was already losing color, if the bleeding didn't stop, then his heart would.

$\mathcal{H}$

Chapter Nine

Charlie marked the tag number on her clipboard and listened as Graham continued rattling off information. She penciled what information he'd given her about each number. Did the cow have a bad back? Bad teeth? How much dosage? Eyes good? She scribbled in a frenzy to try and keep up. The noisy herd expressed their disapproval at the treatment by bellowing and tossing out free kicks for any well-cushioned thigh they could find. Due to this chaotic display, no one saw Calvin ride up until he yanked Graham's shoulder back to spin him around. His blue eyes were frantic as he tried to catch his breath. He held his phone up in the air and threw it down in anger as he gripped the front of Graham's shirt. "Answer your phone!"

Graham never lost his control, but instead, gently placed his hands over Cal's as Cal began rambling about Hayes and the accident and the blood. Lawrence walked up, his smile disappearing as he heard the news and he rushed towards his truck, grabbing his own phone and making the call to emergency services.

Calvin rushed back to his horse, Graham grabbing the reins of the nearest one he could find.

"Wait!" Charlie yelled. She looked up at Graham. "I'm a nurse. I have a first aid kit. Let me grab it and come with you."

"Hurry."

Charlie sprinted into the house, the screen door slapping behind her as her grandpa, mid sip, fumbled his cup at the abrupt interruption. "Hayes is hurt!" Charlie screamed over her shoulder as she ran to her room and began searching in the back of the closet for her medical bag. She grabbed it and made for the door again, her grandpa catching her by the shoulders.

"What happened?"

"He fell off his horse in the ravine. I've got to go." She tugged away from him and when she ran towards Graham, he lent a hand down to her and lifted her up into the saddle behind him. Kicking the sides of his horse, they galloped as fast as they could manage to reach Hayes.

The horses deserved medals after the long ride to the back pasture, Charlie thought. Not only were they winded, but the terrain they had to cover at such a pace meant the Hastings horses were going to have some sore ankles for the next week or so. She would personally treat them to extra treats or oats or whatever for their heroic performance. Calvin pulled up and circled back, pointing to a thicket of trees. Charlie knew which ravine he meant, and her heart rate kicked up a notch. Death Valley. At least, that's what she and her cousins used to call it growing up. They felt like Tarzan and Jane when they were brave enough to swing across it one summer. But the steep drop was over eight feet, and she knew that if Hayes landed on the bottom, he'd be lucky to come out with just scrapes and bruises. Lawrence reached up and plucked her off the saddle as if she weighed nothing, Graham dismounting behind them. All sprinted after Calvin.

"Seth!" Cal's voice called out. "Seth!"

"Down here!"

Charlie raced towards the sound of his voice and reached the edge of the ravine as Lawrence did. Lawrence muttered a gasping, "Sweet Jesus" as they looked down at Hayes.

Graham never stopped to look. He immediately rushed to the edge and fumbled his way down, stumbling at the bottom and landing on one knee, a blow Charlie knew rattled his entire body and would need its own treatment after this. Lawrence gripped one of her hands as Graham stood at the bottom and intercepted her halfway by lifting her over the remaining distance to the ground and setting her on her feet. Cal tossed her bag to Graham, and they hurried over to Hayes. His coloring was white, his eyes closed, his breathing labored. Seth held a blood-stained t-shirt over his leg and looked up in relief when he saw Charlie. She placed her fingers against Hayes's neck, relieved that his pulse was there, though slow.

"I didn't know what to do," Seth reported, his voice quiet so as not to disturb Hayes. "There was so much blood. I just tried to stop it. I—"

Charlie gently reached for his hands and removed them from Hayes's leg. "It's alright. You did good. Just back on up for a minute and let me have a look." Her voice was calm, her smile tender as she watched the wide-eyed youngest brother fall back on his haunches to give her space. She lifted the once blue and white checked pearl snap and braced herself. Sure enough, a compound break to the femur threatened Hayes's life. She noticed the bleeding hadn't completely stopped, due to lack of pressure. But she couldn't blame Seth for that. He was probably terrified of injuring his brother further. "Come here." She motioned for him and despite his fears, he leaned forward as she fished in her medical bag and withdrew a clean towel. "We have to stop the bleeding. It's almost there, but we need to put some pressure on it."

"But he'll scream."

"I don't think he will. He's passed out." She grabbed Seth's hand and rested it on the towel above the break in Hayes's thigh. "One hand here," she instructed. "And the other here." She placed his other hand below the break. "I want you to put some pressure on." She pressed his hands down to show him how much and then began pulling other items out of her bag.

"Emergency should be on their way," Lawrence called down. "I was able to get a call out before riding out. Phillip stayed behind to direct them here and to get calls out to the family."

"How's it looking?" Graham asked. "What can I do?"

"We need to make a splint. Even though emergency services are on their way, they're going to have to stabilize his leg before transporting him anywhere. If we can do that for them, they can get him out of this ditch quicker."

"What do you need?" Graham asked.

"I've got what I need, but I need your hands."

He knelt beside Hayes, avoiding Seth's hold so as not to jostle his brother and waited for instruction. Charlie tapped on both of Seth's hands to lighten his pressure and lifted the corner of the towel. "Looks like the bleeding has stopped. That's good." She rested her fingers to Hayes's neck. "We need to cover him. His body is starting to go into shock."

"What does that mean?" Seth asked. "Wh—"

"Blankets, Seth," Charlie ordered.

He yelled up at Lawrence and Calvin and the brothers dug out what they could find from horses. Two saddle blankets appeared at her elbow. "Not exactly the most sanitary, but it's the best we can do. We have to keep the wound as free of contamination as possible. Cover his chest and arms." She folded Hayes's arms across his chest so they would be tucked under the heavy blanket Graham spread over him.

She made quick work of bracing two wooden rods on either side of Hayes's thigh and wrapped with clean gauze strips as tight as she could muster. She rested the towel over his leg.

"What now?" Graham asked.

"Pray." Charlie sat next to Hayes, her fingers lightly resting against his neck again as she monitored his pulse. Judging by the amount of blood the brother had already lost, she was surprised he was hanging in there, but if the helicopter didn't come soon, she wasn't sure how much longer Hayes could make it. She looked at Graham's stoic face, Seth's worried eyes, Lawrence's grim mouth, and Cal's pale complexion. Not one brother dared look away, not one offered words of encouragement or hope, not even Seth, as they all waited on bated breath for the sounds of a chopper. Charlie felt the deep whoosh of relief when she heard the distant sounds of helicopter blades slicing through air.

~

"Mi amor?" Ali's panicked voice carried into the waiting room of the hospital in Fort Stockton as she rushed inside holding Ava on her hip, the little girl's arms wrapped tightly around her neck. Her wide brown eyes beckoned Julia forward as she removed Ava gently, and despite her own giant tummy, held the girl and walked her over to a chair and sat. Annie intercepted Ali and gripped her hands. "Now, he's in surgery, Alejandra, and they have the best doctors workin' on him. Charlie made sure of that." Ali's wild eyes landed on Charlie who sat in the far seat, her shirt and pants covered in blood. "Como es ella?" Ali asked quietly.

"She's doing okay." Annie squeezed Ali's hand and offered a tender smile. "She saved his life."

Ali walked over to Charlie, Charlie immediately hopping to her feet, expecting to be yelled or screamed at. What she wasn't expecting was for Ali to throw her arms around her in a tight embrace. She rocked back on her heels and hugged Ali in return. "Gracias. Gracias. Thank you. Gracias," She muttered over and over. Charlie tugged back and gave a weak smile.

"He's strong, so I have high hopes that he'll be just fine."

Alice and Ruby rushed into the room next, Alice's hair windblown from what must have been a run through the hospital parking lot. Ruby rushed directly towards Lawrence and into his arms, grateful for his safety, but already shaking from nerves and the thought of something happening to Hayes.

"What's the word?" Alice asked. "What have they told us?"

Annie shook her head and Alice's face crumbled. "He's gone?" Her face paled and Annie stepped forward in a hurry.

"No, no, no, honey. He's not gone." Annie grabbed her hands. "We just haven't gotten any news since he went back for surgery. Charlie said they swept him right in when they landed."

Alice spun around and narrowed her eyes on Charlie. "You." Anger deepened her cheeks and had her storming towards Charlie. "If your old, nasty grandpa would have taken better care of his responsibilities and his ranch, then this never would have happened!" Her voice began to rise as her finger pounded into Charlie's chest. "It's your fault! Hayes might die and it's entirely your family's fault!" Her eyes glassed over and regret filled her face, but she didn't take her words back as Calvin swooped in and pulled her towards him instead.

"Hay is going to die?" Ava's little voice squeaked up at Julia and Graham reached over and tugged Julia and Ava into his arms. "Not on our watch, kiddo."

"He's supposed to be my daddy." She began to wail and Ali, torn between comforting her daughter and needing her own comfort, melted into a chair and sunk her face into her hands. Phillip walked over and pulled Ali into a warm embrace.

Charlie stepped towards the exit as if contemplating escape, but Seth intercepted her. "Don't leave," he whispered. "She's not really mad at you. Alice just has to have someone to lash out at."

"But she's right." Charlie's eyes swam as she looked up at him. "It is my fault. None of this would have happened if I hadn't agreed to accept your help. If I hadn't needed help."

Seth placed his thumb under her chin and lifted her eyes to his. "Stop that. Everyone feeling sorry for themselves or being mad at each other isn't going to help Hayes. You helped him the best way you knew how, and without your help he *would* have died. So stop that whinin', right now."

Her back stiffened. "I'm not whining." Appalled, Charlie took a step back and he shook his head.

"Nope. You're not going anywhere. You're staying right here with us. Because even when the doctors come out to update us, we will need you here to interpret all their medical jargon."

"I'm sure there are other nurses that c—"

"You're stayin'," her grandpa's voice interrupted her, and everyone's heads snapped up at his presence.

No one moved, not even Bob Chandler, as he stood awkwardly holding his hat in his hands.

Graham slowly stood to his feet and walked towards the man, Seth's eyes bouncing between the two to wager which one would end up swinging a fist first. But instead of a fist, Graham extended his hand and Bob, though hesitant at first, shook it. "Thanks for coming." Graham motioned towards a free chair. "He's still in surgery. We don't know any updates yet."

Bob nodded a solemn greeting towards Annie, the woman biting back any rude comments as Henry walked into the room carrying a tray from the cafeteria with cups of coffee for everyone in the room. His feet stopped in their tracks when he spotted Bob, but he offered him a cup as well and continued on his way.

It was then that Seth realized Charlie was resting her head against his chest and her arms were wrapped around his waist. He hugged her tighter and rubbed some warmth and encouragement back into her body.

H

Chapter Ten

No news was good news, Charlie repeated to herself as she dipped her gloved hands into the freshly tilled garden and picked out the large rocks that seemed to dapple the surface. She tossed one into the wheelbarrow, the resounding thud satisfying. She hadn't heard from any of the Hastings family since she had left the hospital over four days ago. Hayes had made it through surgery, but he'd not only had the compound break to his femur, but an additional two broken ribs, a concussion, and lost more blood than the doctors liked, so he had quite an extensive hospital stay ahead of him. Maybe that's why she hadn't heard from anyone. He was still in the hospital, no new update. She pulled another rock from the garden and tossed it without even glancing up. Thud. "You mad at that wheelbarrow?" Her grandpa's voice interrupted her work, and she didn't have the energy to plaster on a forced smile and handle whatever conversation or argument he wanted to start. She continued working. "There's someone here to see you." She paused and turned on her knees. Seth stood, hat in his hand, face tired, but wearing a warm smile.

"Need some help?" he asked.

Surprised, she remained on her knees in the dirt as he nodded his thanks to her grandpa, who to her surprise, left without a qualm. Seth knelt beside her and surveyed her work. "You're making good progress, though I'm afraid you missed your planting window. You didn't plant the seeds I gave you, did you?"

She pointed to a row of five-gallon buckets along the back porch, fresh seedlings sprouting.

"Smart. Container gardening is a good start until you get this finished. I don't know why I didn't think of that." He fished his hands in the row and sifted out the rocks and tossed them into the wheelbarrow.

"How's Hayes?" she asked, nervous about the answer.

"He's good. Already smiling and happy to be alive. Thanks to you. He'll be laid up for a while, which will be interesting to see how he handles that. But your grandpa, after he left the hospital, has tended to the horses while we've all been back and forth, so Hayes didn't have anything to worry about there.

"I'm surprised Grandpa did that. He's been avoiding me the last several days."

"You sure about that? Or are you avoiding him?" She narrowed her eyes on him and Seth held up his hands to ward off the barbs she shot his way. "I'm just askin'. Don't sass me with those blue bullets either. Your grandpa has been... surprising."

"He seems the same to me."

"I think you've buried your head in this garden the last few days, then. He's been over at the 7H every day tending the horses."

Astounded, Charlie stopped in her own sifting. "What?"

"Yeah. I've had some good conversations with him lately. He's not half bad."

"He stepped foot on the 7H? Willingly?"

Seth laughed. "Yep. He and Graham have been discussing some partnerships too."

"Like what?"

"With the cattle. Maybe even some hunting. I see you're speechless." Seth tapped her chin to close her mouth. "Also, I offered to help in that regard. Hunting season is here, so Clint and I will be surveying your mule deer, whitetail, and elk populations to see what you guys can offer as far as hunting packages. Your herd combined with ours might give us both a successful season. There are some details that need to still be worked out. Lodging, cooking, cleaning and what not. But it'll come together. Clint has a passion for this kind of stuff, so he'll see it done."

"And what about you?" she asked. "Is it your passion?"

"Hunting?" He shrugged. "I enjoy it. Some would say I love it. But I don't think it's my passion. My heart lies in the overall scheme of things. I've shadowed Graham too long not to love every aspect of ranching. I love the entire operation; seeing what needs to be done and creating a path to get to the finished product or operation that's desired. I've watched Graham do that my entire life. I've watched Hayes do it with the horses, Phillip at the feed store, and Clint with our hunting operation this year. Calvin has a passion for the machines... any machine. And Lawrence, well, he's a bit like me. We like it all. So yes and no, to the passion question." He grinned and went back to working.

"I've been looking around this place the last few days," Charlie admitted. "And wondering how in the world I could possibly bring it back to life and trying to gauge if I have enough passion to do so. My heart was always medicine. Now?" She shook her head. "I don't know if I have it in me to stay here anymore. Seeing what happened to Hayes made me rethink things. How could I possibly ask people to come risk their life on this place just so I can whip it back into shape and back into operation? Seems selfish."

"No, it's not," Seth challenged. "Ranching and farming and hunting can never be selfish. It's impossible. Taking care and grooming the land and livestock benefits the very ground you walk on, the air you breathe, the food you eat, even the very clothes you wear. People forget that. What we do is important. Does it provide us a living in the process? Hopefully. Sometimes yes, and sometimes it seems like more of a headache than a blessing, but it provides. The land provides. A healthier habitat for wildlife, lush grazing lands for livestock, and fertile farm ground take time to develop. We've been at it my entire life and *still* have pastures that need brush control work. But the more we pour ourselves into establishing new grazing lands, the larger cattle herd we can have. The more cows we have the more we can produce for the market. Feed people. Clothe people. Put nutrients into the soil."

Her face softened as he spoke because she could see the passion reflected there.

"What?" He flushed when he realized she sat staring at him and he was babbling.

"I'd call that passion."

Chuckling, he nudged her shoulder with his hand. "For what it's worth, seeing you so intense and professional during Hayes' accident, I was thankful you were a nurse. But seeing you dig in this dirt, the work you've accomplished on this overgrown mess, I think if you put that much intensity into running this place, I have no doubt you'll make it a success. And it seems like your grandpa is willing to start making some steps that direction as well. I think he's received an honest and open look at the conditions of the place. Graham's been... well, ain't nothin' subtle about Graham." Seth laughed as she did. "And he's been rather upfront with Bob about it all, so I see a little positive light ahead. Don't know how far off it is, but it's there flickerin', sayin' 'Charlotte. Charlotte. Save me. Save me.'"

She burst into a laugh at his high-pitched whisper in the air and tossed a handful of dirt at him. He brushed a hand over his chest to wipe it away and grinned.

Sighing, she looked to him and reached down a hand to help him stand up too. When he did, he towered over her. She looked up at him, liking the fact that the sun shined behind him, and that shadow shielded his face under his hat so she couldn't see his eyes. He gently tugged her towards him. "Can I tell you something else?" he asked, his voice hushed.

"What?" Her heart hammered in her chest as he placed her hand over his chest. She felt the same erratic pace beneath her palm that she did in her own chest. Wondering what he planned to say wasn't even on her mind now. All she wanted to know was if he was about to kiss her. Because she wanted him to.

"I think you're a pretty awesome person, Charlie Chandler, and I think you're the prettiest girl I've ever seen."

His head dipped and his lips brushed nervously over hers, soft and sweet, tender and slow. A throat cleared and had Charlie hopping away as if stung by a bee. She saw her grandpa and Graham both standing on the edge of the porch, arms crossed, both looking unimpressed by what they'd just witnessed. Seth's neck turned pink up to his ears as he nodded his farewell to her and walked towards his older brother. Graham's lips relaxed into a smile when Seth reached him, and they both turned to walk back towards his truck parked out front. Bob Chandler, however, stood with his eyes still focused on Charlie. As much as she wanted to shrink under that hard stare, she couldn't help but turn her face to watch the brothers walk away. And she was glad she did, because at the last minute, Seth turned and offered a friendly wave, tipping his hat in farewell, and her heart leapt into that now familiar, frenzied pace.

~

Seth shifted on the ground, his legs cramping from sitting too long in the same position as he waited patiently for the day to break. Clint sat atop a hill in the neighboring pasture watching and waiting and hoping what they'd seen on the camera footage the last few weeks actually showed up at the feeders. On camera, the mule deer were consistent every single morning, but it was always different when boots were on the ground and actively watching and hoping for them to show up. It was also still a bit warm. The temperatures had dipped in the mornings and evenings, but it was still a far cry from cold. November would come soon enough, though, and the temperatures would fall, and he couldn't wait. Clint was more excited than he was, his older brother all but giddy when the temperature dropped one degree less than the previous day. Seth smirked at the thought, his binoculars drifting towards the property line between the 7H and Chandler's Crossing. He hadn't heard from Charlotte in over a week. He hadn't visited her either. To be honest, he was trying to steer clear for a bit just in case Bob Chandler wanted to string his hide up the nearest tree for kissing her. So far, Seth was still alive, but he was also nervous. Graham didn't seem to care, but Bob... Seth's pulse jumped in nerves. Yeah, he'd keep his distance for a bit until he felt he could safely make the trip. Then he'd go and check on Charlie again. He was crazy for thinkin' he had a shot with a Chandler. Was that what he was after? A shot with Charlotte? Yes. Deep down, he wanted to know her more. He wanted to help her. He wanted to see the rift between Hastings and Chandlers mended. Not that he expected everything to change overnight, but he never understood why such hatred had to last from generation to generation in the first place. He rarely held a grudge against anyone. He couldn't fathom holding one for fifty years or more like Bob Chandler.

He spotted several good-sized mule deer around the feeder and sent a quick text to Clint about his findings. His phone buzzed and he answered. "Yeah?"

"How many?" Clint asked.

"Four."

"That's it?"

"For now. More might come. How many have been showin' up at this feeder?"

"Eight or more."

"Then I'll wait."

"Nah, they've normally already come and gone by now. If they're not there, they've moved to a different one." Clint huffed a breath. "Guess I'll sit tank #3 next."

"And me?"

"You can pack it in if you want. If you're lucky, you'll hit Graham's house about the time Julia's cookin' breakfast."

Seth's stomach gave a low growl at the thought. "Now that would be a good start to the morning. I think I'll do that. Later." He hung up and shouldered his backpack, zipping his binos in the front pocket as he walked. He texted Julia to make sure it was okay if he stopped by for a warm meal. He didn't want her to feel obligated or to overdo it for him. She texted back a happy invitation that made him smile and thank the Lord he'd brought Julia into Graham's life. Into all their lives. And with the promise of a hot breakfast, it didn't take long before he was pulling up to Graham's house. Julia sat on the front porch sipping a cup of decaf tea. She waved.

"Well? A good morning?"

"Somewhat. Not to Clint's liking, but it's always a good morning when you get to see at least a little wildlife. Graham up?"

"Of course." She grinned. "He's in the kitchen making breakfast."

Seth's brows rose. "Really? He know I'm comin'?"

"I informed him." She patted the rocking chair beside her. "Keep me company during my banishment."

"Banishment?" Seth asked. "What could you have possibly done?"

She laughed. "Graham doesn't want me on my feet, therefore, he has taken over all cooking duties now until the baby comes."

"Wow." Seth, impressed with his brother's chivalry, frowned when he saw Julia's annoyed expression. "Oh. I'm guessing you don't like that?"

"Well, I mean, I do, but I don't. I'm not helpless or delicate. I'm just carrying a baby. I can stand and make breakfast, for goodness' sake."

Seth smirked. "He's being a bit overprotective, huh?"

"Somewhat." Julia smiled. "It's sweet."

"But annoying," Seth added for her, and she gently rubbed a hand over her stomach.

"It's for the best." Graham walked out carrying two plates. One for Seth and one for Julia. "I keep telling her she'll be thankful for a rest once the baby comes, so she better enjoy it now."

"You mean you're not going to take over all nightly duties with the little one?" Seth asked.

Graham's stoic expression never changed as he said a strong, "No."

Julia and Seth both laughed at his honesty.

"Good luck, Jewels." Seth took a hearty bite of his eggs and thanked Graham around his mouthful. His brother walked back into the house to fix his own plate.

"So have you talked to Charlie?" Seth asked Julia.

She nodded. "I did yesterday, actually."

"How's she doing?"

"You could ask her yourself," Julia suggested with a wink.

Seth felt the heat climb up his neck and he avoided her gaze.

"I think she likes you," Juila encouraged. "Or she seems to. She asked about you." His head popped up and had her stifling a giggle. "Said you left the other day after a good conversation, but she hadn't heard from you since."

"I was giving her some space."

"I see. From what?"

Seth waved his hand around the air. "Everything. Things have been a bit intense lately what with her coming to the ranch, us working with Chandlers, Hayes gettin' hurt, me kissing her, and—"

"You kissed her?" Julia's voice rose in excitement as Graham walked out of the house and immediately turned back around and went back inside, as if uncomfortable with the topic.

"I figured Graham told you. He saw me do it."

"He didn't. Graham Hastings!" she yelled, and her husband poked his head out the screen door. "I can't believe you didn't tell me Seth kissed Charlie."

Graham looked at Seth and shrugged. "Wasn't my business."

"It most certainly is." Julia tossed a bit of scrambled egg at him. "Or it should be."

Seth chuckled as he took a crunchy bite of bacon.

"So, you kissed her and then you haven't talked to her?" Julia asked.

"I was letting her think about it."

"And protecting his hide," Graham muttered, ducking back inside the house.

"That too."

"Bob was here yesterday afternoon," Julia explained. "Seems there's going to be some changes coming to Chandler's Crossing here soon."

"What do you mean?" Seth asked.

"I heard him tell Graham that he will be meeting with a landman from Creek Bottom this week."

Seth's jaw dropped. "About what?"

Julia shrugged. "Not sure. Whatever it was about, though, Graham wasn't too happy about it."

"Interesting." Seth finished his breakfast in silence, contemplating what Julia had just shared. If Creek Bottom Mineral Company offered enough money, would Bob Chandler sell out? Would he jump ship all together? That thought worried Seth. It would worry all of them. He needed to talk to Charlie.

H

Chapter Eleven

"So that's it?" Charlie watched as her grandpa waved farewell to the landman as he drove away. He stopped short of the porch when he saw her disappointed gaze and stubborn stance. "You're done? The ranch is done?"

"No decision has been made yet. He just made an offer."

"One that you're actually considering?"

"I'd be a fool not to."

"Grandpa, you can't sell the ranch. It's been in your family for— well, since God created the earth. You can't just throw it away."

"I hardly consider his offer throwing it away."

"But what of your legacy? Great-granddaddy's legacy? If you sell, it'd be like all your work was for nothing."

Bob's eyes sparked as he walked one worn boot up after the other and cleared the steps to head inside the house.

"Sure. Walk away from me. Leave me in the dark. As usual," Charlie barked after him. "I don't even know why I try with you anymore. Why did I try at all?" She crossed her arms over her chest, leaned back on the porch swing, and tried to will away the tears that started brimming. One betrayed her and slid down her cheek before she hastily swiped it away, fresh anger making her eyes sting even more. How could her grandpa just throw in the towel? She'd left her career, her life, her friends to be here on the ranch and keep it in the family, and now he just wanted to hand it off as though none of that mattered?

The screen door creaked as Bob stepped back out onto the porch and held out a fresh glass of sweet tea in a handled mason jar. She didn't move. "Take it," he insisted, his gravelly voice not holding his usual bite.

Charlie accepted the tea and took a sip to calm herself down, but pretended the overly sweetened brew didn't taste as good as it was. She was not going to give him the satisfaction. She was mad, dang it. Furious even. He had no right to hold such a meeting without her knowledge, not now that she was here and part of the ranch. But he had. So, no. She wouldn't just sit here and sip exceptional sweet tea and pretend her feelings weren't hurt. She was spitting mad and he had a right to know.

"What he's offered," her grandpa began, "would keep you, your parents, your cousins, your future children, and possibly even your future grandchildren quite comfortable. They won't have to work this ranch to scrape by. They could have anything they'd want."

"And that's what you think we all want?" Charlie asked in disgust.

"It's what a lot of them want, yes."

She knew it was true. She she hated that it was, but her other family members would probably jump at the chance to be rid of the ranch and capitalize on its worth. It was a shame, but the truth. The oil industry in all facets loved land, and her grandpa sat on a goldmine. "What did he offer?"

"Enough."

"That doesn't answer my question." Charlie shifted to face him as he sat next to her. "They want a quarry?"

"That seems to be the plan. Though it doesn't quite matter what they do with it if they buy it. It will be theirs."

"And you're okay with that? Just giving our land away for some cash after you've worked your entire life on this place?"

"I'm old. I don't have enough years left in me to get this ranch back in full operating order like it used to be. And that's on me." He looked down at his weathered hands and his thumbs brushed away the condensation on his own glass of tea. "But I also don't want to force family to take care of the place when none of them want to."

"I want to," Charlie declared. "I moved here to help you. I moved here to learn."

"Out of necessity. Not because this is what you want."

"How do you know what I want, Grandpa? You've never asked me," Charlie challenged. "And if you think I'm just willing to throw away this place, you're wrong. This is where my memories of Grandma are. It'd be like throwing her away. And what about this house? They'd more than likely tear it down. I can't see that happen. Not when I can do something to stop it."

"Charlie," Grandpa reached over and patted her hand. "I don't think you realize how much work it's going to take to whip this ranch back into shape. The Hastings boys weren't wrong in their assessments. I've let it slip too far."

"No. You haven't. And you know who has shown and taught me that? Seth Hastings. He believes this place can be great again, and he's even made me believe it. And made me want to see it that way again too."

"Well," Bob stood and walked towards the front door. "I'm going to consider the offer. Weigh my options. I'll let you know when I make my decision."

Deflated, Charlie rocked back and forth on the swing. The easiest option would be to sell the place, but the hardest option would be to sell the place and see her family's legacy and history disappear. She didn't like it one bit. She wanted to keep Chandler's Crossing under the realm of a Chandler, and she was ready for that responsibility, even if she had to prove herself to her grandpa, her family, or to everyone.

~

"You going to be staring off into space all day?" Lawrence asked. "Because if you are, I want to switch partners."

Seth sighed and shook his head. "Sorry. I've got a lot on my mind."

"You?" Lawrence chuckled. "What could possibly have you all twisted up?"

"I've got problems too sometimes," Seth admitted. "I just don't always share them."

"Alright, well, tell me, then. What's got you daydreamin', cowboy?"

"Chandler's Crossing."

"Ah. Got a thing for Charlie Chandler, huh?"

"No, that's not it. Well... yes, I do, but that's not what's bothering me. Julia mentioned Bob Chandler is talking to Creek Bottom Mineral about selling out."

Lawrence dropped the square bale of hay in his hands and looked at Seth in surprise. "No way. There's no way Bob Chandler would sell that ranch."

Shrugging, Seth lifted a bale and placed it on the trailer behind Lawrence's truck. "Well, he's been approached. I verified all this through Graham. Graham said he's seriously considering it since he doesn't have someone in his family interested in taking it over."

"I thought Charlie was."

"She doesn't count, apparently." Seth rolled his eyes. "Granted, she doesn't know what all it entails, but yeah, Bob isn't taking her seriously."

Lawrence went about his business, readjusting the stacks so as to squeeze a few more bales into place. "You talk to her about it?"

"Not yet." Seth hopped down off the trailer and helped Lawrence reorganize the hay barn before they both hopped into Lawrence's truck and headed toward storage shed closer to the pasture where they'd house their cattle for the winter months. The hay was only supplementary if the grass disappeared too quickly, or if they got snow. "I thought about going over there again today, but I don't want to pry into something that may or may not be my business."

"It kind of is," Lawrence assured him. "We live next door. A rock quarry is going to disrupt wildlife around here. That impacts us."

"How concerned do you think Bob Chandler is with the Hastings family?" Seth scoffed. "Not at all, I'm thinking."

"Graham said he wasn't so bad now."

"Yeah, because he feels guilty about Hayes, who, by the way, is already going stir crazy at his house. We need to take him for a ride this evening."

"I think he's more upset Ava decorated his cast with pink hearts and unicorns," Lawrence grinned.

"You kidding me?" Seth laughed. "He was showing it off to everyone last night at supper. Annie was thrilled." Seth fished in his pocket as his cell phone jingled and he held it up for Lawrence to see the screen. Charlotte Chandler. He swiped his finger to accept the call. "Hey Charlie, how are you?" He liked that even before she said a word his heart did a funny dance in his chest.

"Hey, Seth. I'm doing okay. Listen, I was wondering if you would want to meet up for supper later this evening. Maybe at Sloppy's in town?"

"Dinner?" Seth asked, turning a cheeky grin towards his brother. Lawrence playfully nudged his shoulder in congratulations. "Yeah, I'd love to."

"Great. See you at six?"

"Six is great. See you then." He hung up and punched the air with his fists in a celebratory hoot.

Laughing, Lawrence steered them towards his house instead of the hay shed. "Calm down, Romeo."

"You kiddin' me? The prettiest girl in Parks just asked me to dinner. I can't calm down. Where you going?"

"Back to the house."

"Why?"

"Because it's already close to five. If you're wanting to shower and gussy up before your big dinner, you better get to it now so you have time before you're supposed to be there."

"Thanks, bro. Always lookin' out for me." Nothing could dampen Seth's mood. Even the thought of Chandler's Crossing and Bob Chandler potentially selling could not tamper the excitement he felt over talking with Charlie more. Maybe she'd share more of what was developing over there with him. He hopped out of Lawrence's truck before it had even rolled to a stop, his brother shaking his head on a laugh as he sprinted into Lawrence's house and to his room.

He showered in record time, and he didn't slow down until he sat at a small table for two at Sloppy's Diner. Ruby sat across from him. "You look fancy," she complimented.

"Meeting Charlie here in a bit."

"I see." She smirked. "Lawrence already texted me."

"No secrets in this family. I'm too excited to care."

Ruby hopped to her feet. "Here she comes," she whispered. "I'll be back in a few minutes for your order. Good luck."

Seth stood as Charlie walked to the table. He fumbled over the hug, side-hug, cheek kiss combination he tried to pull off, but it didn't seem to bother her as she sat with a friendly smile. "Good to see you."

"You too." She relaxed her shoulders as Ruby slipped by silently and placed menus on their table before rushing off again. "She's good," Charlie chuckled as Ruby overheard the compliment and waved over her shoulder in thanks. "Thanks for meeting up with me."

"Sure. No problem. I was glad to." Seth tried to calm his nerves, but his legs bounced under the table from the jitters. "How are things over at Chandler's Crossing?"

"Could we talk about a less complicated subject?" She grimaced and leaned forward, her hands under her chin. "I think Grandpa is going to take an offer from Creek Bottom Mineral and sell the place."

Seth's heart lurched in his chest. "No way."

"Yep." Her eyes watered and she cleared her throat to shake away the sudden flood of emotion. "I don't like it, but he seems pretty resolute. I'm leaving Friday."

"Wait—" Seth held up his hand. "Leaving? As in going back to Dallas?"

"Why stay? I won't have a home anymore if he sells. And I don't want to be here when it does. I want to remember it as it was and is."

"But did you tell him you planned on taking over? That that's why you're here?"

"Until I was blue in the face." She shook her head. "It didn't matter. He thinks he's doing me a favor by accepting their deal."

"And he's selling it all? Not just considering surface rights? Or just a portion?"

"All of it," she confirmed. "It makes my stomach sick thinking about it."

"Yeah, mine too. I can't believe this." Irritation laced his words and she reached across the table and squeezed his hand.

"I wanted to tell you in person that I was leaving and hang out with you one more time before I left. I've appreciated your help with the garden and with... everything. For believing and supporting me, as well. I'll never forget it."

Growing bitter at the turn in their conversation, Seth appreciated the interruption by Ruby, until he saw her pale face. "What's the matter?"

She nervously wound her wash towel in her hands. "Julia."

Seth immediately hopped to his feet.

"They're taking her to Fort Stockton. The baby is coming."

"It can't be. She still has six weeks!"

"I know." Ruby untied her apron. "Give me a second and we'll ride together."

Seth looked regretfully at Charlie.

She waved him on. "Go. I'll be fine... Uncle Seth," she offered with a sad smile.

"We'll meet up one more time before you leave. Yeah?"

"Sure," she replied, her noncommittal offer driving a knife through his chest.

He grabbed her face and placed a firm kiss to her lips, pulling back to stare down into her pretty face. "We will, Charlie. We will."

Ruby darted towards them and offered a sympathetic smile towards Charlie as she tugged Seth towards the door, and they sprinted to his truck. His belly twisted into knots over Julia's predicament, Charlie leaving, Chandler selling. Seth wasn't sure he could take another blow.

H

Chapter Twelve

Packing her suitcase gutted her. She hadn't realized how heart-wrenching it would be to leave the ranch. But she needed to. She didn't want to wait around for a phone call from Seth or another meet up. She wanted to depart on his kiss. A kiss that still had her reeling hours later. Her Grandpa wasn't going to change his mind. It was time for her to leave. It was time. She placed her makeup bag on top of a pair of jeans and remembered those were the jeans she wore the first time she met Seth Hastings. Funny how she remembered the exact outfit she wore: Pink plaid shirt, jeans, her Lucchese boots, and her horseshoe necklace for luck. She remembered it all. She even remembered what he wore and how his smile tilted slightly higher on the left side and how his eyes always seemed to dance when he was in a good mood. They hadn't been dancing when he'd kissed her at Sloppy's. No, they'd been serious, sharp, and breathtakingly blue. She'd remember that too, along with the disappointment of never knowing how things could have turned out between them had she stayed. But she wouldn't find out, and she'd just have to chalk that up to her grandpa, along with the long list of other grudges she planned to hold for the rest of her life. She closed the suitcase and walked downstairs. Her grandpa glanced up, his eyes shocked to see her all packed up.

"I guess you'll call me when it's all done? I'm assuming there will be a family meeting?"

"You're leaving?"

"Well, yes. No reason for me to stay and run a ranch if there is no ranch to run." She knew that was a petty comment, but she couldn't help it. She was ticked off and she wanted him to know it.

"I see. It's not that I don't appreciate your willingness, Charlotte. It's just... time."

"Sure. Whatever you say. You're the owner, so you can do as you please. But I don't have to be here to see it disappear, so I'm headed back to Dallas. I'm going to be at mom and dad's house for a bit until I can find another apartment and move my stuff out of storage. Get another nursing job. I emailed my old boss, so maybe that door is still open."

"And that's what you want?" her grandpa asked.

"Guess it has to be, right?" She pulled her suitcase to the front door and left it there as she gave him a brief hug. "Thanks for giving me a shot, Grandpa. I'm sorry it didn't work out."

"Charlie, now I don't think you need to rush off like this."

"I'm not rushing off. It's time. If you decide to get rid of any of Grandma's things, let me know. I'd like to have some of it." She saw he hadn't even thought that far ahead and his face blanched and then turned sad. "Take care, Grandpa." She walked to the door, grabbed her bag and walked out.

The tears started falling as soon as she reached the bottom step, but she didn't stop. She shoved her suitcase in the trunk of her car, closed the door with more force than required, and hurried to hop inside when she saw her Grandpa's silhouette walking towards the door of the house. She didn't want to talk anymore. It would only make her leaving harder. On him and her. Her phone dinged with an incoming text. Seth. A tear splashed the screen as she opened a picture of his tired face as his family all waited to see if they'd have a Hastings niece or nephew. They'd been at the hospital overnight, anxiously waiting, and she prayed Julia and the premature baby would be healthy and fine. She responded with, "Patience," and he replied with a smiling emoji. She hoped he would let her know what Julia ended up having, but she had a deep-seated fear he wouldn't speak to her again after he realized she'd already left town.

Her phone rang again, and she saw her grandpa's name pop up on the screen. She sent it straight to voicemail. She couldn't talk to him right now. She couldn't talk to anyone. She was just sitting, parked at the end of the long drive, her car pointed towards out of town, but she hadn't moved forward yet. She wanted to take her time. Say goodbye to the place. She wished she'd had time to ride around on horseback one more time.

A truck turned into the ranch entry and paused, the white insignia on the driver's side door causing her blood bubbling. Creek Bottom Mineral Company. The man rolled down his window with a charming smile and he tipped his hat. "Ma'am. I'm here to meet with Bob Chandler. He around?"

She nodded. "At the house."

"10-4. Thanks." He dipped his head and continued on his way, and she watched as the trail of blowing dirt disappeared from view.

Should she turn around? Should she sit in on the negotiations? No. She wasn't asked. Her grandpa planned to handle it on his own, like he did everything. He didn't need her help, which he'd made very clear over the last few months. The one time she tried to help, she almost killed a man. Hayes Hastings would be fine if she'd never tried to take matters into her own hands. Lesson learned. She shifted into drive and with one last look at the front gate, left.

~

"I've got ten bucks saying Graham will either pass out, vomit, or scream at the doctor." Clint offered the wager to Phillip, and to everyone's surprise, Phillip put money on the same.

"Now, you two stop that," Annie chided. "Your brother is at his wits' end worryin' about Julia and the baby. Bless his heart. The last thing he needs right now is his brothers makin' silly bets behind his back."

"I'll put ten down for vomit." Calvin forked over his cash and Annie gaped at him completely ignoring her command. Clint grinned and added it to the pot.

"Seth?"

Seth looked up from his phone, disappointment clouding his face at not receiving any response from his last text to Charlie. She'd answered the first, but not the last two. "What?"

"You want to place a bet?" Clint repeated.

"Oh, no, thanks."

"He's too busy stalkin' his phone for a text from Charlotte Chandler," Lawrence baited.

"I'm just worried," Seth mumbled, Annie lightly patted his hair. "That girl is fine. She's lived with Bob Chandler for over four months now. If she can handle that man, then she can handle anything." Helena walked up to Annie and handed her a fresh cup of coffee. "Thank you, sweetie. Now you may want to hover by Phil; Clint is turning him into a gambling fool. Where is Alice, Cal?" Annie fretted.

"She had to go deliver a breech baby calf over in Sheffield this morning. I imagine she's on her way by now, though."

"She will want to be here. Julia would want her to be."

"She'll be here, Annie." Cal looked up at the movement from the corner of his eye. "Hey-o! Look who it is." He hopped to his feet as Ali pushed Hayes in a wheelchair into the waiting room, Ava riding on his lap, holding a fluffy purple unicorn. Hayes beamed, though his face was pale and beads of sweat had begun to dapple his forehead.

"Hayes Matthew," Annie clucked forward. "What on earth do you think you're doing? You are to be on bed rest, young man."

"I tried to tell him." Ali shook her head. "But he insisted."

"Makin' poor Alejandra lift you in and out of the car and into this chair." Annie glowered at him.

"Oh, I didn't," Ali assured her. "Alice helped. She was coming in from Sheffield and we... well, we gracefully tried to get Hayes in the car. The staff here helped get him out of the car."

"It's a big day," Hayes defended his decision and gladly accepted the capable hands of Ruby to pluck Ava off his lap. Ruby carried Ava towards a small table with coloring books and crayons.

Graham walked into the waiting room looking worn out and nervous and everyone fell silent.

"Well?" Henry asked. "What do we have?"

"No baby yet," he reported. "Contractions are coming closer together now. Doctor seems to think within the hour. Julia's tired, but she's adamant she doesn't want an epidural or anything to help her along."

"Atta girl," Lawrence cheered her on. "Tough cookie you got there, Graham."

Annie gave him a firm hug and an extra squeeze, her hand gently resting on his cheek a moment as she murmured words only meant for his ears. Then she hugged him again before a nurse stepped into the hallway and called for him. Graham's long legs reached the nurse in record speed, the woman's eyes slightly amused and impressed at his jumping to action. She nodded towards the rest of the family as if to encourage them as well.

Alice rushed into the waiting room, a bouquet of flowers in a glass vase and a grouping of balloons bouncing in her face and everyone she encountered along the way. "Is it here? Did I miss it?" She wore two different shoes and her shirt's buttons were askew, but no one mentioned it as she set the vase on one of the side tables and sought out Calvin. He gently tucked one of her flying fray hairs behind her ear and kissed her. "No baby yet, Al. You're just in time."

"Good Lord, how long does it take Julia to have a baby?" Alice looked at her watch. "I Just knew I'd missed it." Breathless, Alice sat with a flop, her long day catching up with her. She looked at Seth next to her. "Why are you mopey?"

"I'm not." Baffled, he just stared at her.

"You look like it. This anything to do with Charlotte leaving town?"

"What?" Seth asked.

"Yeah, I passed her on the way home. She told me she was headed back to Dallas."

"Right now?" Seth asked.

"Well, like a couple hours ago, yeah." Alice glanced at her watch again and then shook her wrist. "I let this battery die. I need to charge this sucker more often."

Seth hopped to his feet and walked down the hallway, dialing Charlie's phone. On the second ring, she answered. "Hey, Seth." He could hear the sounds of driving in the background.

"Alice said you left Parks."

A hesitant and reluctant breath blew through the line. "I did."

"I thought we were going to meet up one more time before you left?"

"I decided it was time."

"Oh really?" Heat flared up his neck and into his cheeks and the Hastings temper that rarely ever blossomed in Seth came rushing out full force. "So you decided to change our plans without telling me? You decided to sneak off?"

Defense had her tone sharpening. "I'm not sneaking anywhere. I told you I was leaving Parks."

"Yeah, but in like a week or two. Not today."

"I made the decision that was right for me."

"That's bull. You're running away because you don't want to see Bob sell out. I don't blame you there, but we still have time to convince him not to. I thought we were going to fight this. Together."

"It wasn't going to happen, Seth. Grandpa made it clear he was selling. As I was leaving, the landman was pulling into the ranch to finalize things. It's over and done."

"Do you want the ranch, Charlie?" Seth countered.

"Of course I do. You know I do. Why are you even asking me that?"

"Because you're giving up too soon. I know it." Seth ran a hand through his hair. "Turn around."

"Excuse me?"

"Turn around. Come to the 7H if you have to. You can stay with Alice, but don't leave yet. I think I have an idea that maybe, just maybe your grandpa would go for."

"Seth, look, I appreciate this, but it's over. And I'm sorry... well, I'm sorry that I won't be around to be... whatever it is you're wanting me to be."

"I'm wanting you to run that ranch, Charlotte Chandler." He heard a sniffle in the phone and his anger fled. "Turn around, please," he insisted, his tone softening. "Give me one more Hail Mary. Literally, for all our sakes, give me one more shot."

"I'm already three hours away."

He could hear the smidgen of hope in her voice, and he smiled, his entire body relaxing. "Turn around anyway. I'll meet you at the ranch."

"But Julia?" Charlie asked.

"Is about to have her baby any second. I'll be there when you get to the 7H," he promised her.

"Alright. I'm turning around. But Seth, if your family wants you there, I don't want you rushing back to the ranch and missing out on experiencing the birth of your first niece or nephew. I'll wait until you get there."

"Promise?" he asked.

"I promise. Though I have no idea what you have up your sleeve and I'm doubtful it will make a difference, but... I'm just hoping it will."

"Thank you, Charlie. Thank you. I won't let you down." He hung up and turned to find Calvin, Lawrence, Phillip, and Clint leaning against the walls of the hall with their arms crossed, and a curious Hayes rolled up, blocking a quick escape with his wheelchair.

"That's an awful big promise." Calvin narrowed his eyes on Seth. "What do you have rolling around in that head of yours, Seth?"

"A plan to save Chandler's Crossing."

"Unless you have millions of dollars packed away, I don't see how that's possible," Lawrence warned.

"I have an even better idea. And it will work. For everyone."

"Everyone?" Clint shook his head. "I sense a partnership coming on, and that ain't going to work. You know it won't. Not with Chandler."

"Not a partnership." Seth gritted his teeth and clenched his fists. "You've got to give me a shot too. I can talk to Bob Chandler, and I think he'll like what I have to say."

"If you believe in your plan, so do we," Graham's voice interrupted them and had them all jolting to attention when they turned and saw him standing and holding a tiny bundle in his big arms.

"What the—" Lawrence peered over Graham's shoulder, lightly hugging his brother as he peered down at the tiny face. "Look at that," he whispered. "Good job, bro."

"I'm only allowed a minute or two and then I have to go back, but Julia wanted everyone to see."

"It's so tiny." Clint gently rested his giant hand on the baby's hospital cap-covered head. "What is it?"

"It's a baby, doofus." Lawrence swatted Clint upside the head as the others laughed.

"It's a girl." Graham's voice held wonder. "A baby girl."

"A girl," all the brothers said in unison, all with a touch of fascination in their tones.

"She's beautiful, Graham," Phillip congratulated. "Tiny, perfect, and beautiful."

"Graham, honey." Annie drew their attention to the nursing crew waiting for Graham to bring the baby back into the room. Annie lightly kissed his cheek. "Proud of you, sweetheart. You're going to be an awesome daddy to this sweet baby girl."

"You mean Annie Ruth," Graham corrected her. "This here is Annie Ruth Hastings."

Annie's eyes misted as she held a hand to her heart. "My name and your momma's name?"

"Yes ma'am. Figured if she was to rule the roost, she needed to have the names of the two strongest women I knew."

"Mr. Hastings." One of the nurses gently tapped his shoulder.

"Right," Graham cleared his throat and bit back emotions no one had ever seen cross his face. "Thank you all for being here."

"You take care of Jewels for us, Graham." Phillip smiled. "We'll hold off on all the visiting until you guys get home."

Lost in his baby girl's face, Graham only nodded as he allowed the nurse to guide him back down the hall.

"And he's a goner." Alice grinned. "Amazing what a little lady will do to a tough fella." She hip bumped Ava standing next to her and winked down at the little girl as she drew yet another heart on Hayes's leg cast. Ali's hands rested on Hayes's shoulders, the three of them a cute family already.

"I can't wait to see Ms. Julia and her baby together." Ava's dreamy eyes had Hayes tugging her ponytail in fatherly affection as she went back to drawing.

"I guess I need to buy a baby gift now." Calvin rubbed the back of his neck. "Now that we know it's a girl."

"You haven't gotten the baby anything yet?" Alice asked.

"Well, no." Cal flinched at the punch to his arm. "We didn't know the gender. I didn't want to buy something yellow either. You know how I feel about yellow."

"All you boys can buy that sweet baby girl something and have it waitin' for when Julia and Graham come home with her in a couple of days. Right now, I suggest we all go home and get some rest."

"Ruby Cole," Lawrence called towards Ruby as she sat with Helena hovering over one of their phones, already online shopping for baby Annie Ruth. Ruby's head popped up. "You ridin' with me?"

"Is that you asking?" she challenged, her hands resting on her hips.

Looking chuffed, Lawrence flushed. "I want you to ride with me. I'm leaving. Would you please join me?" He forced the last line out and his brothers chuckled at his awkwardness.

Ruby rewarded him with a chummy grin and a kiss to the cheek. "See, that wasn't so hard, was it?"

Seth looked to Alice. "It alright if Charlie spends the night at your place tonight?"

"My house in Parks or the guesthouse on the ranch?" Alice asked. "Because Jimmy still occupies my Parks house."

"Guesthouse."

"Sure. Why?"

"Long story. I just need a place for her to stay the next few days."

"I thought it was just for tonight," Alice reminded him.

"Hopefully so, but I'm not really sure. That okay?"

"It's fine." Annie walked up and placed a hand on his shoulder. "Go do what you need to do, Seth. Like Graham said, we'll back you with whatever plan you have in that head of yours. We don't want to see that ranch sold, even if it means schmoozing with Bob Chandler the rest of our lives."

"I assure you, Annie, there will be no schmoozing." Seth grinned and gave her a quick kiss on the cheek. "I'll let y'all know how it goes." He hurried out of the hospital, dialing Charlie once he reached the parking lot. "I'm on my way, Charlotte."

H

Chapter Thirteen

Charlie sat on the front porch of the tidy little guesthouse on the 7H Ranch. A fish out of water, she tried to comfort herself with an orange tabby cat that had graced her with his presence and insisted she rub his belly. She obliged, of course, because who turns down such a cute companion? However, she felt his attention was more to disrupt the dogs that were penned next to the house, as they barked almost constantly at the smug cat as it stretched and swished his tail across the lawn, in front of their pen, and on towards Charlie. The smugness made her smile as the cat rubbed against her leg, and

Charlie swiveled her finger in its tail as she saw Seth's truck come up the drive. Relieved she no longer had to sit outside, but sad her time of quiet had come to an end, she stood to her feet. He hopped out of his truck and rushed to her, pulling her face to his and kissing her with pent up frustration, angst, and interest. When he pulled away his actions clearly took himself by surprise and his big round eyes made her laugh. "Good to see you too, Seth."

Horrified, but also not disappointed in landing a good kiss, Seth tried to play it cool. "I, uh, hi Charlie. I'm glad to see you."

She stepped towards him and placed her hands on his shoulders gently pulling him into a warm hug. "Me too."

He kissed the top of her head. "Now, let's get going. I want to catch your grandpa before supper time."

"Are you going to fill me in on this great plan of yours?" she asked, allowing him to tug her towards his truck.

"Nope." He flashed a grin over his shoulder and opened the door for her. She climbed inside, liking the way his truck smelled, and began buckling her seatbelt, finding it amusing and a little pleasing to see her hands fumble with the task because he'd set her nerves on fire.

When he slipped behind the wheel, Charlie reached over and placed her hand on his before he could crank the engine. "Seth," She waited until he looked at her. "Whatever happens, thank you for the Hail Mary."

Nodding, his face sober, he turned the key, and they silently made the short drive to Chandler's Crossing. She could see her grandpa's truck parked in its usual spot under the shed, but he wasn't out on the porch and the house looked still. "He's home at least," she murmured. They climbed out of the truck and at the sound of the doors shutting, Bob Chandler's head poked around the side of the house where she'd been grooming the garden plot. He stepped around the house, holding a shovel, and Seth groaned. "If he buries me alive, please tell my brothers where my body is."

Their nervous eyes met, and she forced a smile. "Good luck."

"Charlie." Her grandpa's voice held surprise. "I thought you left."

"I did." She thumbed towards Seth's direction. "But this guy insisted I come back to hear him out."

"About what?" Bob asked.

"Well, sir, I'll tell you, but I'd be a whole lot more comfortable if you put that shovel down."

Bob's lips twitched, but he obliged by leaning it up against the side of the house and motioning towards the porch. "Let's sit." Bob sighed as he sat and watched as Seth let his granddaughter have the other free rocking chair and took a place on the top step, removing his hat and twiddling with it in his hands. "Well? What do you have to say, son?"

Seth took a deep breath. "Hire me."

Charlie and her grandpa both pulled back as if slapped.

"Excuse me?" Bob asked.

"Hire me," Seth said again. "As your foreman."

"And why would I do that?"

"Because you need me. You need someone to turn this ranch around. And I can do it. I've spent my entire life on the 7H, sir. Ranching is in my blood. I've shadowed Graham since I could walk, much to his dismay half the time." Seth smirked thinking of all the headaches he'd given Graham over the years. "I know how a successful ranching operation should run. Now, I know it will take time, and I know we can't implement changes all at once, but I think with time, we could turn this place around. And I'm willing to do it."

"And you'd give up living on your family place?" Bob asked.

"The truth is, Mr. Chandler, I've struggled with really finding my spot over there. I haven't even built my house. I've had a spot ready to go for over a year and I haven't bit the bullet because I just wasn't sure if I was meant to be there. Now I know why. I'm meant to be here, helping you, sir. My brothers support me in this. And they'll support this ranch. I know you may not like us, but... we're decent folk. We have our heads screwed on right, thanks to Annie and Henry, and we're honest. I'm honest. And I work hard. And I listen. I'm the youngest of seven, I've always had to listen, so I am open to learning from you about this place and what you've done in the past and what you would like to see happen for the future."

"Seth—" Charlie flashed a quick glance at her grandpa's serious face.

Seth held up his hand for her to hold off on commenting because he wasn't finished. "I know money is tempting. I know the value of this place too, so I'm sure Creek Bottom has offered you a pretty penny. I can't say I'll ever be able to earn what they're offering you. But I can help keep this land in your family's name. Charlie wants to be here, sir. And she deserves to be. She doesn't know how to run a ranch, I get that, but I do. And what I don't know, I can learn from you and Graham. Charlie can learn from all of us. And soon, sir, you will have someone to hand this place off to. To a Chandler. Hell doesn't have to freeze over for a Hastings and a Chandler to get along."

"And you'd work for me?"

"Yes sir."

"Some say I'm not easy to work for." Charlie's heart sank. She knew that was true. Everyone did.

"You know, I reckon I heard a rumor or two." Seth smirked and Bob Chandler bit back a gruff laugh. "Sir, I'll be honest with you. Graham isn't always a peach either. I love him, but he's a tough man at times. And he's hard to work for some days, but we love what we do, and our goal is the same: to provide the best care for the land, livestock, and wildlife that we can. Groom it, graze it, clean it up, preserve it, produce on it, and live on it. So with respect, sir, I think I can handle working with you. We may not see eye to eye all the time, but all I'm asking is that you respect me, and I'll respect you in return."

"You sure are offering a lot."

"I am. Yes."

"And you'd live here, on Chandler's Crossing?"

"Yes, sir."

"And you'd be comfortable taking orders from Charlotte when the time comes for her to run the place?"

"Yes, sir."

Bob turned and looked at Charlotte. "What are your thoughts on this?"

Charlie nodded. "It could work. I'm willing to give it a shot."

"And this has nothing to do with the fact you're sweet on my granddaughter?" Bob asked.

Seth's cheeks deepened in color, but his eyes remained steadfast and honest. "No sir. I mean, I am sweet on her. I'll be truthful about that. But Ms. Charlie has a decent head on her shoulders. And one thing I've learned in the ranching community is that when someone is willing to learn the business, you don't shut them down. There's too few willing to learn and embrace this lifestyle, so when someone is, I say train them and work with them. I'm willing to do that with Charlie. And if things don't go smoothly, I have a place I can go. But I want to see Chandler's Crossing rejuvenated so that Charlie can be where she wants to be, and another ranch doesn't disappear because there's no one willing to run it."

"Anything else?" Bob asked.

Seth shook his head. "Not that I can think of right this minute. I sort of didn't expect to get this far, so I'm afraid I'm a bit unprepared now."

Chuckling, Bob extended his hand. "I appreciate your honesty, son."

Seth shook it and then stood to his feet. "I'll let you two discuss this over for a bit." He looked to Charlie. "I can bring your stuff over or leave it. You just let me know." He started down the steps.

"Now, hold on one minute." Bob stood to his feet and Seth waited patiently at the bottom of the steps. Looking at Charlie, her grandpa asked. "You on board with this idea of his?"

"I already said I'm willing to give it a try."

"And you'll live here?" Bob asked in surprise.

"Yes." Charlie nodded. "I'd like to."

The man's eyes grew glassy at her statement, but he focused on Seth. "Then you have a job, Hastings."

Seth's eyes rounded and he looked at an equally shocked Charlie. Slowly, they both smiled and cheered. Charlie jumped into his arms and Seth swung her around. When her feet landed on the ground, they both flushed and looked at her grandpa. His usual serious face held a genuine smile and she rushed into his arms. "Thank you, Grandpa. Thank you."

~

"So now I'm shorthanded all because you went and got a job on a different ranch." Clint pretended to be annoyed, but his smile reflected those of his other brothers as well.

Julia sat in the recliner rocking Annie Ruth as Graham rubbed his chin. "I will admit, this wasn't exactly what I was thinking as a solution, but if it's what you want, I support you."

"I'll need your help." Seth looked to all of them. "All of you."

"And you'll have it," Calvin replied. "You'll need equipment on that place. We can work out a deal of sorts."

"Thanks." Seth nodded. "Yeah, lots of clean-up is in my future."

"And a crew," Lawrence pointed out. "Chandler given you the go-ahead to hire some hands?"

"Two. I asked Phillip to put a posting up. I hope you don't mind, but I sort of used the Hastings reputation to recruit, even though it's for the Chandler place."

"Smart move," Clint mumbled.

Hayes shifted in his wheelchair and grunted.

"You alright?" Seth asked.

"Fine. Just hating this thing. My butt gets sore after a while. If you need horses for anything or need me to look over Chandler's, let me know."

"And you'll do what?" Graham asked, nodding towards his cast.

"I'll do it when I'm back on two legs." Hayes tapped his cast. "This ain't forever, praise God."

Julia reached over and squeezed his hand. "Hang in there, Hayes." She stood to her feet and all the men stood straighter to be ready to help with whatever she might need. Laughing, Julia held up a finger. "I'm just going to get a glass of tea."

"I'll get you one, Jewels. Rest." Lawrence started towards the kitchen.

"No." Julia looked at Hayes. "I'm about like Hayes. I appreciate being spoiled and resting, but I can go get a glass of tea for myself, Lawrence. Thank you. I need to stretch my legs." She walked towards the brother and lightly kissed his cheek. "You can hold Annie Ruth, though. That'd be helpful." Whether Lawrence was prepared or not, Julia began gently handing the baby over. Nervous to hold such a tiny human, Lawrence tenderly sheltered the baby in the crook of his arm. His smile lit the room.

"Look at this." He grinned. "I'm holding a baby."

"And for the love of God, don't drop her, please." Graham smirked as he watched his brother carefully walk towards a chair and sit. Julia winked at Graham and walked to the kitchen.

"Where will you be living?" Clint asked.

"In the bunkhouse for now," Seth explained. "The entire upstairs is a separate living quarters from the bottom floor, so the hands will live downstairs, I will have the upstairs."

"Decent enough." Calvin looked up as Julia walked back in the room with a tray full of glasses and began handing each of them some tea. Her hostess cap was back in place, and though she was still recovering from having a baby, she glowed with new motherhood and was twice as beautiful.

"And Charlie?" Julia asked. "How does she feel about this new change?"

"She's on board. And I'll admit, I sure do like seeing her every day."

"Don't bite off more than you can chew at one time," Graham warned. "The ranch should be your focus."

"It is, for sure. But I'm also not going to pass up an opportunity with Charlie. I like her. A lot."

Julia slipped her arm around Seth's waist and hugged him. "I have a good feeling about you being over there."

"Just don't upset Bob. You break Charlie's heart, Bob Chandler will shoot you," Hayes predicted. "And trust me, that ravine was not a comfortable place to be tossed into."

"I'll be careful," Seth assured them. He reached for his hat off the arm of the chair Calvin occupied. "I better get back. I'll see y'all at church Sunday."

They watched him leave and Julia's face held a touch of sadness. "I'm happy for him, but I'm sure going to miss having him here."

Graham pulled her into his arms and kissed the top of her head as she sniffled. "These dang hormones," she mumbled and had the men chuckling as they all stood to their feet to go their separate ways.

"You still have all of us, Jewels." Lawrence offered Annie Ruth back to her momma and reluctantly walked away. Clint dipped down and kissed little Annie on her forehead as he passed by.

"I'll mosey on out as well." Hayes wheeled himself through the house and out onto the back porch, the temporary ramp on the stairs giving him access to and from wherever he ventured. Lawrence helped him ease down the ramp and wheeled him towards his truck. Despite his broken ribs, Hayes managed to lift himself on his own and into the passenger side. Lawrence waited patiently.

"I love your brothers," Julia whispered to Graham. "All of them."

Graham kissed her temple.

"You two get some rest." Calvin placed his hat on his head and kissed little Annie as well, brushing his fingertip over her smooth little cheek. "I'll be sitting for Clint this evening. Now that Seth is out of pocket, look who got recruited for hunting season." He pointed at himself. "Alice will be thrilled."

"She does like the look of you in camo. She told me so," Julia encouraged and had him laughing on his way to his truck.

Seth, though having left the house, was watching the farewells, appreciating his family more than ever. He looked at the garden around him and would miss working its rows every day. He knew he left it in good hands with Julia, and he would help with planting each season as he always did, but he'd miss the everyday. However, he and Charlie would create another one at Chandler's Crossing and he'd be able to bring forth new growth and new life to the place. A place that needed that special touch.

H

Chapter Fourteen

The air felt different. It held a touch of fall to it that felt like breathing in a cold front and exhaling the holiday season. Charlie loved it. It would warm up mid-afternoon, but the mornings were for savoring that promise of change. And change was already underway at Chandler's Crossing. Seth had been working at the ranch for only a week, and so far the transition had been smooth for everyone. Even her grandpa walked with a lighter step and hope in his eyes. His mood had improved considerably, and she even caught him sketching plans for a new set of cow pens after supper the night before. He was listening to Seth, he was working with Seth, and he was impressed with Seth. All good things. And Seth respected him in return. She took a sip of her coffee and Seth walked up the usual path towards the house and greeted her with a warm smile. "Mornin'."

"Morning."

"Ready for the day?"

"Almost. Grandpa insisted on making breakfast."

Seth's brows lifted into his hairline as he took the empty rocking chair next to her.

"I know," Charlie said, equally baffled. "And there's enough for all of us, he said."

"Wow."

"It's amazing, Seth. I feel like he's just completely transformed back into the grandpa I remember visiting when I was a little girl."

"I'm glad."

"I owe you more than you can imagine."

"You owe me nothing. Well, except maybe dinner at Sloppy's. We never did have that night out."

She grinned. "Definitely. So, what are you teaching me today?"

"Well, today we're going to take a ride and look at the extent of your brush problem, Ms. Chandler. And we're going to create a plan on how to bring back some grazing lands for you."

"I like the sound of that. And Grandpa?"

"He's riding along with us. I want to hear what's already been done in some of the pastures, if they've been sprayed before or chained or whatever process they used back in the day."

"Smart plan." She smiled at him, then leaned toward him and placed a sweet kiss to his lips. They hadn't kissed since the day he ran up to her at the 7H and she could tell her actions surprised him. "Is that alright?" she asked. "Or have things changed too much?"

"Ms. Chandler," Seth lightly brushed her lips with his again. "I will never turn down your kiss. Never."

She gently tugged the front of his shirt until he kissed her again and then rested her forehead against his. "Maybe we could start every day this way."

Seth rubbed his chin in consideration. "I could probably pencil that in." His grin sobered as her grandpa stepped out carrying two hot plates for them. "Thank you, sir."

Disappointed she and Seth couldn't continue the sweet moment, but thankful for her grandpa's efforts in making breakfast, Charlie accepted the plate with enthusiasm.

"I think I will let you two take the ride today." He handed Charlie a clip board with several pieces of paper and notes attached to it. "This is the information you'll need as you go around pasture to pasture. And room for you to jot down notes that Seth might mention."

"Oh." Charlie accepted the board. "Are you sure?"

Turning away from Seth, Bob winked at Charlie and smiled. "I'm sure. I've got plenty around here to keep me busy. You two better get to it." He nodded at their breakfasts and disappeared back inside the house.

Stunned, Charlie sat a moment.

"What?" Seth asked. "Something wrong?"

Charlie turned to face the door and back to Seth, and then looked at the door again. "I'm pretty sure my grandpa just gave me the go-ahead."

"Well, yeah, he gave you the clipboard, that's huge." Seth dipped his head in congratulations and Charlie shook her head.

"No, I mean, I think he just encouraged me to... well, continue to do what we were doing before he came out here."

"And what was that?" Seth asked, leaning towards her with a smug expression.

Laughing, Charlie nudged his face away. "Seth Hastings, you're trouble."

"It's what I hear." He grabbed her hand and kissed the back of it. "You know, we've never really talked about there being an us. We've just sort of... evolved, I think." He took a bite of his breakfast and shyly avoided her gaze.

"Is this you asking me out, Seth?"

His mouth was full, and she took advantage of his silence and continued. "If it is, the answer is yes. If this is you telling me you think I'm special, then good, because I think you're pretty special too. Not many people could face off with my grandpa the way you did. And if this is you wanting to kiss me," She leaned towards him again and waited until he swallowed his bite and then pressed her lips to his. "Then good, because I want to kiss you all the time."

His hand slid behind her neck, and he claimed her lips in his, leading her further and further over the edge, no longer teetering, but plunging headfirst to being in love with him.

One Month Later

Thanksgiving differed from their usual Sunday dinners at Annie's, because it brought everyone to the 7H and into Graham's house. Though now, the long wooden table that housed him and his brothers growing up was no longer big enough to accommodate his brothers and all the lovely women new to their lives, so, folding tables were set up around the living room as well. Julia and Annie had outdone themselves on creating a warm and inviting environment, with seasonal table decorations and settings. Helena handed Seth a glass of wine when he walked in the back door and welcomed him inside. "The fancy stuff, huh?" He held up the glass, observing the tinted liquid with a suspicious eye.

"It's Thanksgiving. No beer allowed, according to Julia," Helena told him and then offered him a small pastry no bigger than a golf ball.

"And what is this?"

"You'll thank me." She motioned for him to eat it and he popped it into his mouth, his eyes brightening.

"Red velvet cake ball," Helena explained. "They're amazing."

"Thanks." He walked inside and rested his hat on the rack by the door amongst his brothers'. Baby Annie was currently being nuzzled in her Nana's arms. "Grandma sure looks good on you, Annie," he complimented, and Annie looked up with a proud gleam in her eye.

"I adore it. And I adore this baby. Why, I've been completely useless around here since Julia handed her off."

"As you should be. There's plenty of hens in the house to take care of the rest of the details." Lawrence ducked as Ruby swished a towel to pop him on her way by.

"Lawrence Dean, you best keep those kinds of comments to yourself, or they'll kick you out on your rear. And I would hate to see that happen after seeing the wonderful meal they've prepared," Annie warned and then clucked her tongue when the baby started shifting and making soft whimpers.

"How's it going over at Chandler's?" Phillip asked, sitting down on the sofa beside Calvin and accepting the fresh glass of wine from Helena, who took her job as the welcoming committee seriously. She kissed his lips before moving back to the kitchen.

"Been going good." Seth relaxed against the cushions of a leather chair near the fireplace and liked that Graham had lit a low fire to take the chill off the air, but also to add an inviting warmth to the house. "Charlie will be here in a few minutes. I think Bob was a little nervous in coming, so she wanted to give time for them to have a moment."

"What do you think Dad would say about us having Bob Chandler at our Thanksgiving table this year?" Clint asked.

"I think he'd be mighty proud of you boys." Henry walked into the room and took the empty recliner next to the sofa. Calvin held his cup of coffee for him as he situated his position and then handed it back to him. Henry nodded his thanks. "You boys have not only transformed this ranch over the years, but the fact you've stepped up in helping Bob, well, both your parents would be impressed and mighty proud. Mighty proud, indeed. I know I am. Annie too, when she isn't speaking in baby language these days."

Alejandra and Ava entered the house, two pans of chocolate cake immediately taken from Ali's hands by Lawrence to help relieve her load. "Hayes is outside." She nodded over her shoulder. "He'll need some help."

A clatter tapped the door frame and Hayes wrenched open the door, holding it open with one crutch before Calvin hopped to his feet to help his brother out. "No chair?"

"No." Hayes pointed to it at the base of the stairs. "I couldn't sit out in the cold when I could smell what was in here." He smiled in greeting and hobbled his way towards the empty spot on the sofa Calvin had vacated. "And now I'm officially worn out for at least a half hour. Geez I'm ready to feel myself again."

"You are lookin' a bit soft," Phillip teased. "All those sweet meals being delivered by Ali and no exercise."

Hayes patted his still flat stomach and smiled. "I don't mind it one bit."

Graham walked into the room carrying the baby and took a free chair at one of the folding tables, his fingers lightly holding a pacifier in place as the baby attempted to patiently wait for her next feeding.

"I never thought I'd say this, but fatherhood looks good on you, Graham." Clint smiled as his oldest brother lightly brushed his cheek over his baby girl's dark, downy hair.

"Suits him just fine." Henry bounced to attention in his chair as Ava jumped in front of him with a big smile and a picture she'd drawn him. "Well, hey there, buddy bear!" Henry scooped the little girl onto his lap and pointed to the paper. "What'cha got there?"

Ava then began walking him through the stick figures in the drawing, her little voice filling the space as the women continued chatting in the kitchen and preparing the meal. A knock sounded on the door, and Seth stood to greet Charlotte and Bob. "Come on in." He kissed Charlie as he removed her coat and shook Bob's hand. He hung Charlie's coat up and offered to take Bob's hat, the older man's eyes soaking in the large crowd of people.

Graham stood and walked over. "Good to see you, Bob. Welcome. You guys find a spot if you can." He smiled as Charlie leaned forward to peer at his daughter, the tiny baby still a small six and a half pounds.

Seth guided Charlie with a hand at the small of her back towards the kitchen to see the other women, and Annie walked up and embraced her. "Charlotte, you're just in time. I need someone to fill the deviled eggs. Come on, honey." She tugged Charlie into the mix, abandoning Seth in the doorway. She turned and he offered a nervous smile as she fell into place next to Helena at the island in the center of the kitchen. Helena handed her a plastic storage bag full of yellow mixture. "Annie's fancy, you fill them like you're icing a cupcake." She demonstrated and Charlie nodded.

"I'll wash my hands and get started." She walked to the sink, Julia rinsing a large roasting pan. She swiveled the nozzle towards Charlie and smiled.

"Hi, Charlie. I'm so glad you guys came." She offered a gentle squeeze to Charlie's arm. "How's your grandpa in there?"

"Like a fish out of water, I'm afraid."

Sympathy and a hint of determination glinted in Julia's eyes. "Well, we can't have that." She walked towards the open archway between the kitchen and living room, but stopped herself from interrupting when she saw Graham handing their daughter over to Bob Chandler. The older man's large worn hands were tender and gentle as he fawned over the little girl. She leaned against the archway, then Charlie walked up beside her, and a soft gasp escaped her lips. "Babies have this magical power," Julia whispered. "Of turning even the strongest men into cooing, adoring fans."

"I don't know when he's last held a baby." Charlie watched as if seeing a stranger and Seth walked over to drape his arm around her shoulders. "Do you see that?"

"I do." He smiled at Julia over Charlie's head before turning his attention back to Bob. "Welcome to a Hastings Thanksgiving, Ms. Chandler."

Alice breezed into the house, her hair, as usual, blown in various directions, her eyes bright, cheeks pink from the cold, and a store-bought pie in her hands. Her father walked in after her. "Sorry I'm late. Not my fault this time." She motioned over her shoulder to her dad. "This guy was still feeding his ostrich when I got to his house."

Doc Wilkenson shook Graham's hand and hugged an approaching Julia. His eyes settled upon Bob Chandler holding a tiny pink bundle and he did a double-take. Graham gave him a sly wink as the doc headed the direction of the baby and to greet his old acquaintance. Alice inhaled a deep breath.

"Now, I can say I'm glad I showed up when I did, because that smells like lunch is almost ready."

"Dodgin' work, as usual," Clint baited.

"I'm going to let that one slide because it's Thanksgiving." Alice pointed his direction in warning and then popped him on the back of his head as she bypassed him and walked into the kitchen. Over her shoulder she called, "By the way, your woman was pulling up."

Clint hopped to his feet, eager to see Bailey Keller, his girlfriend who'd been on assignment in the neighboring county for over a month. He met her at the door with eager arms and lifted her off her feet as he kissed her.

Henry laughed and shook his head. "I don't know what we've done to deserve all these good women coming into our boys' lives, but I sure do love how our family has grown."

Annie walked into the room and rounded everyone up. "It's time." She nodded at Graham, and everyone stood, Bob handing the baby back over to Julia as he prepared for grace.

As Graham's deep baritone thanked the Lord for food, family, and friends, Seth reached over and linked his fingers with Charlotte's. At the unified 'Amen,' he raised her hand to his lips and kissed the back of it. "I think you're the one thing I'm most thankful for this year, Charlotte Chandler."

"You mean you're not thankful for Grandpa?" Grinning, she accepted the light kiss to her forehead.

"Some days," Seth admitted softly and heard her light giggle at his words. "But mostly you." She wrapped her arms around his waist and gazed lovingly up at him. "I love you," he whispered, watching as his words sunk in and her eyes glistened in response.

"And I you." Her voice cracked with nerves and his tilted grin flashed into a full smile before he attempted another kiss. He didn't get far because Lawrence walked up, nudging him towards the kitchen.

"Romance later, food now." Law continued shoving until Seth and Charlie stood in the serving line, Ava squeezing in front of him on the way.

"Ladies first," Ava reported up at him and had everyone laughing.

Ali hid her embarrassed face as Hayes held her in place next to him. "She's fine," he whispered, letting his future daughter watch as Annie spooned food on a plate for her.

Charlie and Seth fell back beside her grandpa and linked her arm in his. "What do you think, Grandpa?" she asked quietly.

He patted her hand and looked up at Seth, seeing past the boy's last name and years of regret and hatred and said, "I think this is one of the best Thanksgivings I've had in a long time."

Charlie kissed his cheek. "Me too, Grandpa. Me too."

Continue the story with

Coming December 2022

THE SIBLINGS O'RIFCAN SERIES   KATHARINE E. HAMILTON

The Complete Siblings O'Rifcan Series Available in Paperback, Ebook, and Audiobook

Claron

https://www.amazon.com/dp/B07FYR44KX

Riley

https://www.amazon.com/dp/B07G2RBD8D

Layla

https://www.amazon.com/dp/B07HJRL67M

Chloe

https://www.amazon.com/dp/B07KB3HG6B

Murphy

https://www.amazon.com/dp/B07N4FCY8V

All titles in The Lighthearted Collection Available in Paperback, Ebook, and Audiobook

Chicago's Best
https://www.amazon.com/dp/B06XH7Y3MF

Montgomery House
https://www.amazon.com/dp/B073T1SVCN

Beautiful Fury
https://www.amazon.com/dp/B07B527N57

McCarthy Road
https://www.amazon.com/dp/B08NF5HYJG

Blind Date
https://www.amazon.com/dp/B08TPRZ5ZN

Check out the Epic Fantasy Adventure Available in Paperback, Ebook, and Audiobook

U<small>THE</small>NFADING LANDS

The Unfading Lands
https://www.amazon.com/dp/B00VKWKPES

Darkness Divided, Part Two in The Unfading Lands Series
https://www.amazon.com/dp/B015QFTAXG

Redemption Rising, Part Three in The Unfading Lands Series
https://www.amazon.com/dp/B01G5NYSEO

AND DIAMONDY THE BAD GUY

Katharine and her five-year-old son released Captain Cornfield and Diamondy the Bad Guy in November 2021. This new books series launched with great success and has brought Katharine's career full circle and back to children's literature for a co-author partnership with her son. She loves working on Captain Cornfield adventures and looks forward to book two releasing in 2022.

Captain Cornfield and Diamondy the Bad Guy: The Great Diamond Heist, Book One

https://www.amazon.com/dp/1735812579

Subscribe to Katharine's Newsletter for news on upcoming releases and events!
https://www.katharinehamilton.com/subscribe.html

Find out more about Katharine and her works at:
www.katharinehamilton.com

Social Media is a great way to connect with Katharine. Check her out on the following:

Facebook: Katharine E. Hamilton
https://www.facebook.com/Katharine-E-Hamilton-282475125097433/

Twitter: @AuthorKatharine
Instagram: @AuthorKatharine

Contact Katharine:
khamiltonauthor@gmail.com

ABOUT THE AUTHOR

Katharine E. Hamilton began writing in 2008 and published her first children's book, The Adventurous Life of Laura Bell in 2009. She would go on to write and illustrate two more children's books, Susie At Your Service and Sissy and Kat between 2010-2013.

Though writing for children was fun, Katharine moved into Adult Fiction in 2015 with her release of The Unfading Lands, a clean, epic fantasy that landed in Amazon's Hot 100 New Releases on its fourth day of publication, reached #72 in the Top 100 in Epic Fantasy, and hit the Top 10,000 Best Sellers on all of Amazon in its first week. It has been listed as a Top 100 Indie Read for 2015 and a nominee for a Best Indie Book Award for 2016. The series did not stop there. Darkness Divided: Part Two of The Unfading Land Series, released in October of 2015 and claimed a spot in the Top 100 of its genre. Redemption Rising: Part Three of The Unfading Lands Series released in April 2016 and claimed a nomination for the Summer Indie Book Awards.

Though comfortable in the fantasy genre, Katharine decided to venture towards romance in 2017 and released the first novel in a collection of sweet, clean and wholesome romances: The Lighthearted Collection. Chicago's Best reached best seller status in its first week of publication and rested comfortably in the Top 100 for Amazon for three steady weeks, claimed a Reader's Choice Award, a TopShelf Indie Book Award, and ended up a finalist in the American Book Festival's

Best Book Awards for 2017. Montgomery House, the second in the collection, released in August of 2017 and rested comfortably alongside its predecessor, claiming a Reader's Choice Award, and becoming Katharine's best-selling novel up to that point. Both were released in audiobook format in late 2017 and early 2018. Beautiful Fury is the third novel released in the collection and has claimed a Reader's Choice Award and a gold medal in the Authorsdb Best Cover competition. It has also been released in audiobook format with narrator Chelsea Carpenter lending her talents to bring it to life. Katharine and Chelsea have partnered on an ongoing project for creating audiobook marketing methods for fellow authors and narrators, all of which will eventually be published as a resource tool for others.

In August of 2018, Katharine brought to life a new clean contemporary romance series of a loving family based in Ireland. The Siblings O'Rifcan Series kicked off in August with Claron. Claron climbed to the Top 1000 of the entire Amazon store and has reached the Top 100 of the Clean and Wholesome genre a total of 11 times. He is Katharine's bestselling book thus far and lends to the success of the following books in the series: Riley, Layla, Chloe, and Murphy, each book earning their place in the Top 100 of their genre and Hot 100 New Releases. Claron was featured in Amazon's Prime Reading program March – June 2019. The series is also available in audiobook format with the voice talents of Alex Black.

A Love For All Seasons, a Sweet Contemporary Romance Series launched in July of 2019 with

Summer's Catch, followed by Autumn's Fall in October. Winter's Call and Spring's Hope scheduled for 2022 release dates. The series follows a wonderful group of friends from Friday Harbor, Washington, and has been Katharine's newest and latest project.

Partnering with her five-year-old son produced another wonderful book in Katharine's lineup: Captain Cornfield and Diamondy the Bad Guy: The Great Diamond Heist, Book One. Partnering with illustrator, Phillip Reed, Katharine and E.K.P. released the first in series with great success in November 2021 and have rallied together again for book two, with an expected release date in 2022.

Katharine has contributed to charitable Indie Anthologies as well as helped other aspiring writers journey their way through the publication process. She manages an online training course that walks fellow self-publishing and independently publishing writers through the publishing process as well as how to market their books.

She is a member of Women Fiction Writers of America, Texas Authors, IASD, and the American Christian Fiction Writers. She loves everything to do with writing and loves that she is able to continue sharing heartwarming stories to a wide array of readers.

Katharine graduated from Texas A&M University with a bachelor's degree in History. She lives on the Texas coast with her husband Brad, sons Everett and West, and their two dogs, Tulip and Paws.

Printed in Great Britain
by Amazon